Blood, Mud, Sisters & Secrets

A True-to-Life Novelette about Southern Life and Secrets

By
L.L. BROWN

ISBN: 9798218309091

Cover by: Aesha Zahra

Printed in the United States of America

Robinson Anderson Publishing
2150 S. Central Expressway, Suite 200
McKinney, TX 75070

TABLE OF CONTENTS

PREFACE

Everyone in Mercer Parish knew the Devereaux family of Bonaventure. Magnolia, Camellia, and Azellia were the daughters of Vacherre and Amellia Devereaux. The Devereaux sisters were strong, independent women who ran one of the most successful corn plantations in the South. Being the oldest, Magnolia was much like her father: stern, logical, and all about the business. Although she was conservative in her thinking, whatever it took to make sure the family business thrived was of the utmost importance to her. Camellia, being the middle child, was much like her mother. She was spiritual and compassionate and really wanted to do as little as possible with the business. Her focus was on helping her students achieve their highest potential, and as far as she was concerned, Magnolia and Azellia could run the business while she remained a silent partner. Although Azellia was the youngest, she was bossy and always had to have her way. She was also very ambitious. She and her two older sisters had continued with their parents' legacy, making invaluable contributions to the continued growth of the corn plantation. But now, Azellia had discovered other interests besides the family business.

With the matriarch passing on to glory, decisions have to be made. Will Magnolia, being the oldest, allow Azellia to have her way and make these important decisions without a proper family feud? Camellia knows that she must take a stronger stance with her sisters if the family is to work together toward the common goal of ensuring the Devereaux family business continues to strive and be successful. Will her spirituality and faith be enough to keep peace? Will Azellia's new life take an unexpected turn and be the driving force of reuniting sisters long estranged, bringing life and love to both families? Or will it tear them apart? Will all of the sisters be able to move forward and learn from the mistakes of the past, or will those mistakes overtake them? Will reuniting these two families build stronger bonds or wedge deceit between them all? Is time what they need, or will the sisters' reunion bring about joy and peace and leave the past as a distant memory?

The answers to these questions are about as clear as mud... and sisters!

PART ONE

CHAPTER 1

"BLOOD"

The Devereaux family had raised corn for nearly eighty years in Louisiana. Vacherre[1] Devereaux and his wife Amellia were a very distinctive couple. He was the great-great- grandson of Maynard Devereaux, a powerful plantation owner during the 1890s, who acknowledged his mixed children with his cook and secret "wife" Pandoralise. Pandoralise[2] was a beautiful and reserved woman of Haitian descent. She captured Maynard's heart the moment he saw her. She became Mistress of the House, and she and Maynard had a long life together. They started the foundation together for what would become one of the most prosperous plantations in the area. Maynard was a generous slave owner who made sure all of his descendants shared in the Devereaux's history and fortune.

---

1 Pronounced *Vash-a-ray*
2 Pronounced *Pan-dor-a-lease*

The Devereaux fortune involved producing corn. Corn was one of the most versatile and lucrative crops to have. Maynard and his brother, Mason, owned one of the largest and most successful corn plantations in the state of Louisiana. When Maynard's brother died, with no family of his own, he became the sole owner. Maynard and his "wife" built Devereaux Plantation into an empire that he passed to his children and their children through the generations. When Vacherre was a young boy, he would work in the fields with his grandfather and father. He was the only one who really had an interest in working the crops. So eventually, when Vacherre's father passed, the plantation became his. He and his wife, Amellia, applied the same work ethic as the generations of Devereauxs who came before them and continued to have success with the corn plantation. From providing corn to the markets and ranchers for livestock feed to food corporations making cooking oil, the Devereaux Corn Plantation was the source of their generational wealth.

Amellia Fontenot was a beautiful woman of small stature. She was the only daughter of Dr. and Mrs. James Fontenot. Her father had been a very prominent doctor in Bonaventure for many years, and Amellia was highly educated. She attended Xavier University and held a degree in Elementary Education. Amellia met Vacherre while attending a gathering for students involved in Civil Rights. She was very soft-spoken but a strong advocate for the cause. Vacherre was highly intrigued by her and asked her for coffee one day. After talking for hours, he asked her on a formal date, and they were married six months later. Amellia was a bright and promising teacher for five years. However, she chose to be a housewife once their first child, Magnolia (Maggie), was born. Later, she gave birth to two more beautiful daughters,

Camellia (Mell) and Azellia (Zell). While raising them, she also worked on the Devereaux Plantation by helping her husband and hosting some of the most exquisite events for the elite of Mercer Parish. Amellia was known for her impeccable style. She was a beautiful spirit with the heart of an angel.

Vacherre Devereaux was a shrewd businessman who, for years, led the 180-acre Devereaux Plantation. He built it into one of the largest and most successful corn farms on the entire Southern border of the state, and he and Amellia ran it together until his death. Being the oldest, Magnolia had learned everything from her father and was made CEO after his passing. She had spent many long days conversing with him about the financial future of the plantation. He stressed to her that it was to remain in the Devereaux family with a Devereaux at its helm. Magnolia, along with her sisters, knew and understood the wishes of their father, and they all vowed to follow his wishes. No matter what, the Devereauxs would always have ownership of the plantation.

Amellia believed her girls were special and possessed "gifts" uniquely to them. She nurtured those gifts as best she could, given that Vacherre did not approve. Amellia came from a long line of spiritual "doctors." She studied the cards and always watched the changing of the moon and the position of the stars. She believed the moon's changing was a significant sign of the path of a person's life. The position of the stars lit that pathway and guided their journey. However, Vacherre was not a believer in signs. He believed whatever happened in life was a direct consequence of behavior, not some spiritualistic mumbo jumbo. He did not want Amellia to fill the girls' heads with that "sort of nonsense." He felt it made them not trust their own ability to succeed.

IIn spite of this, Amellia was very strong in her belief and the "practice." She had quite a lineage. Her grandmother was considered to be a witch of sorts. However, her practices were always for good. She would help folks with anything from headaches to financial hardships. Folks from all over the parish would come to "get help" from Amellia's grandmother. Whatever their problems and ailments were, she always had the perfect cure. As a result, Amellia became a student of the old ways. She had old Southern beliefs and practiced what she preached, but usually in private. However, she would always tell her girls they carried blood and the spirit of tremendous power and strength. They had the capability of being and doing whatever they set their minds to. Collectively, they were a force to be reckoned with, and Amellia made sure they understood the power of their gifts.

Growing up, the three sisters were debutantes in high society. They each had their own ideas and views on everything. But at the same time, their one commonality was the corn plantation, and ensuring that it flourished and carried the Devereaux legacy throughout Louisiana.

Magnolia was a tall, caramel-colored woman with auburn hair, which she always kept in a braid or bun. She never let her hair down, both literally and figuratively. Magnolia earned an accounting degree from Xavier University and was a CPA for one of the largest accounting firms in New Orleans. She was involved in some of the area's largest business mergers and was very successful in her profession. When the accounting firm started downsizing, she decided to bring her talents home. She took over the financial aspects of the Devereaux Plantation. She was very protective of the family assets and made sure that good, sound decisions were made. She was a strong, intelligent, and savvy businesswoman who was ALL about the business. She had little room for anything other than her family's empire and certainly had no room for any type of foolery. Magnolia could be very aggressive and stern. She was a no-frills, bare-bones type of individual. If the conversation was about something other than making money, she usually had little to say.

Camellia, the second daughter, favored her father's great-great-grandmother, Pandoralise, down to her sweet beauty mark on the corner of her left eye and her smooth mocha-colored skin. She often felt out of place, being the darkest of the three sisters. However, she was undoubtedly the most beautiful of the three. Her deep reddish brown locks were stunning and framed her face perfectly. She followed in her mother's footsteps and was a dedicated teacher. She obtained her credentials from Dillard University, where she completed a double major in Education and Sociology. She was the twelfth in a long line of teachers in the Devereaux clan and was well respected in and around Bonaventure. Amellia would often say that Camellia was the most compassionate of the three sisters. She possessed a soothing and level spirit and was always the calming factor in any chaos. She also meditated and studied astrology. Like her mother, she believed in the signs more than the other two sisters. She knew the power of prayer and meditation and always leaned on the Spirit for guidance. She had little interest in the plantation business and tried to stay clear of Magnolia's and Azellia's conversations concerning it unless her involvement was absolutely necessary.

Azellia was the baby girl. Physically, she was Amellia made over. She had long, dark, wavy hair with striking light brown eyes. She had her mother's creamy cocoa-colored skin and her laugh. She was a surprise to Vacherre and Amellia, being almost four years younger than Camellia and six years younger than Magnolia. Azellia was a rambunctious child, constantly pushing the envelope and figuring out how to get her way, especially with her parents. She wanted to leave the state to attend college and escape the deep South and EVERYTHING THAT IT MEANT. She had researched all of the local, historically Black colleges and felt that Howard University offered her just what she was seeking. She begged her parents to let her go up north to attend Howard University. Vacherre had to be convinced to let his baby girl go so far away from home, but he came around, and off to Washington, DC she went. At Howard, she studied law, with her field of expertise being corporate law. She brought everything she learned back to Bonaventure and the Devereaux Plantation. She was a powerful negotiator, and if she knew anything, it was how to bring a group together on common ground to achieve success. She was brilliant and ambitious, and even though she was sought after by many corporate businesses in the area, she chose her family's business and became their lead attorney.

Unfortunately, she and Magnolia were like oil and water. With Magnolia being so "old school," and Azellia being so "modern in her thinking," as Magnolia would always say, they butted heads often. But in the end, they would find common ground. Camellia hated being in the middle of the disputes between her sisters. She sometimes felt isolated and uneasy. She respected Magnolia for her strong sense of family and always wanting to protect their father's legacy. She also appreciated Azellia for being so strong and independent and knowing precisely what she wanted from life. But the most essential thing to Camellia was family. All she wanted was to be there for her students and, above all else, her sisters. When things seemed out of order, she always relied on her faith and sometimes meditated for hours. Meditation always brought clarity and peace and gave her what she needed to communicate effectively with her sisters. She knew how and when to approach them in order to get the best outcome.

The sisters were thick as thieves when they were growing up. They always stuck together and protected each other. They were best friends. However, Magnolia was *always* the boss. They enjoyed being with their mother and hearing the stories of their ancestors and everything they passed down through the generations. Although Vacherre would forbid Amellia from "teaching" the girls her old ways of thinking and believing, they would sneak with their mother down to the old hammock by the water's edge to burn sage, sing, and "practice" by the moonlight. Amellia would make sure Vacherre was away from the house. She did not want to hear him ramble on about his disbelief in the signs. Vacherre was not a spiritual man. He always put logic ahead of any sort of sign or belief in spiritual powers. But, although he did not believe in Amellia's teachings, sometimes he would give way to the fact that there actually could be a power available to Amellia and the girls that he could not logically explain

Once the girls grew older and went on their own paths, their closeness seemed to dwindle. Magnolia and Camellia remained close, but Azellia did whatever Azellia wanted to. She became distant from the family and the ways of her mother's teachings. Plus, leaving Louisiana changed Azellia. She was exposed to so much more than "bridges and bayous," as her mother used to say. She liked the life that living in Washington, DC, had shown her. She had always wanted a husband and a family, while the other two sisters were content in their lives as they were. But would this difference in lifestyles cause a fracture in their relationship? It would come to light one way or the other, and Azellia would have to do her best negotiating to win this one, even if it meant her sisters would lose!

CHAPTER 2

"LEGACY"

It had been six years since Vacherre passed. Magnolia and Azellia were holding true to their father's wishes. Together, they revamped the processes and daily functions of the plantation, adding new systems and over twenty more employees. The plantation was truly thriving. Several other corn farmers had offered a nice lot to the Devereauxs to sell. The plantation was on prime land and produced a significant corn crop every year. Amellia had practically given the reins over to Magnolia and removed herself from the day-to-day operations of the plantation. However, any decisions made about the future of the plantation would have to be agreed upon by all three sisters.

Unfortunately, Amellia's health was declining, and the sisters knew it was only a matter of time before they would no longer have their mother with them. Until then, it was their duty to make sure that Amellia had the best care and was comfortable until her Lord and Savior called her home to be with her beloved Vacherre. Amellia, being the spiritual being she was, was also well aware of her remaining days above ground. She spoke candidly to her girls about what she wanted regarding her final wishes and the plantation.

Amellia looked directly at Azellia as she spoke. "I loved this old house, but not everything that came with it. There were hard times and great times, but my soul was never quite at peace. I sacrificed a lot to help your father keep this place running productively and I do not want you girls to do that. There is enough money to sustain all of you. Do not hold on to the business if it starts to overwhelm you and consume your lives."

Azellia felt every word her mother said. But it appeared that Amellia's confession did not phase Magnolia. It was as if she already knew what her mother was about to say. Amellia instructed Magnolia and Azellia to sell the plantation to the right person and not the highest bidder because it was important that the *right* person had the plantation. Even if it meant someone other than a Devereaux. She continued to emphasize to the girls that the plantation consumed her and Vacherre's life. She spoke about how everything they did was centered around the plantation and making sure that their customers were completely satisfied. They worked hard to ensure that they always produced the best corn crop in Louisiana.

Although the plantation was their life-long focus, she did not want it to be her daughters. She wanted them to live their lives. She wanted them to travel, see the world, and find happiness. She wanted them to see more than just bridges and bayous. She expressed this to them several times. The sisters grappled with the fact that their father vowed never to sell the plantation to anyone while their mother's wish was to sell. However, the sisters understood and agreed to abide by Amellia's final wishes.

There was only one other Devereaux they knew of: Vacherre's cousin who lived in Georgia. She was a successful doctor and had no interest whatsoever in the plantation. She made that abundantly clear when Vacherre passed. Besides, she had no claim to the plantation and was not about to give up her life and successful career to come to Louisiana, of all places!

Azellia had studied the contracts and financial reports for weeks. The plantation was at a point financially where selling would be an excellent financial move. The Devereux Corn Plantation provided corn to over forty suppliers. The customer base was strong, and the profit margin was high. If selling were an option, this would be the prime time to do it.

She figured out a plan. However, she knew it would have to be fail-proof before Magnolia would consider it. She knew that Camellia would agree to whatever Magnolia wanted, which made her main concern Magnolia. Although Magnolia was CEO and made sure that the plantation ran smoothly each day, Azellia was the one working and building successful partnerships with customers. Azellia loved the plantation. But, if she could present Magnolia with a successful plan, they could sell. She could move and live the life she had dreamed of since leaving Washington, DC.

Camellia was on summer vacation and stopped by the Devereaux Plantation to visit her mother. She knew the other two sisters would be occupied with the business and that she would be able to spend quality time with her. Amellia was happy to see Camellia. They sang and talked until Amellia was tired and needed to rest. Camellia loved singing with her mother. It made her sad to see the decline in her eyes. Singing always seemed to lift her mother's spirit, and Camellia and her sisters had voices of angels. Singing was also one of Amellia's legacies to them. Amellia would always hum *Blessed Assurance*, her favorite hymn. She sang it every Sunday at church until she could no longer attend due to her health. Camellia kissed her mother on the forehead and told her goodbye. Amellia was asleep by the time Camellia made it downstairs. She enjoyed her visit and left feeling fulfilled and happy, but also knowing with distinct knowledge that her mother's transition was nearing.

Within a week, Azellia was ready to present her plan for selling the plantation. Magnolia called a meeting with the sisters to discuss the plantation's future and what they should do. They all acknowledged that selling was probably the best decision, and it would honor their mother's last wish. They were all still young and had their own lives to live. Selling the plantation would present all three sisters with new opportunities and endless possibilities for their future.

Azellia presented her plan to both of the sisters. However, she felt it necessary to address Magnolia directly. "Maggie, I have worked hard on this plan, and I am very certain it is the best plan for us. I hope you will just have an open mind and listen."

Magnolia matter-of-factly stated to Azellia, "Well, I am here to listen. I do trust your knowledge. You have always been thorough in every aspect, so I will listen. However, we ALL must agree in order to move forward."

Azellia explained the business plan to improve the plantation. She pointed out that within four years, they would be at a competitive edge. They could sell the plantation and walk away with three times the profit. Magnolia understood the numbers well. After more discussion and more graphs, Magnolia agreed with Azellia's plan. Camellia also felt it would benefit them all. So, she also agreed, making them united in their decision. They would borrow the money needed to improve the plantation and sell it after four years. To seal the deal, they did what they did when they were growing up.

They formed a circle, held hands, and repeated three times, *"If it is to be, it shall be, show us so that we can see."* For as long as they could remember, their mother would always end their "secret" gatherings down by the river with those words. Every time they heard her pray, she would always end her prayer with them. Those words held the belief that if something were meant to be, it would be, and the Spirit would lead them to the right decisions. The chant was passed down from Amellia's great-grandmother, who was an avid student of the cards and stars. She relied on the universe and its signs to show what was ahead for us on our spiritual paths. Amellia shared her great-grandmother's beliefs and knew how important it was to carry it down to her girls.

The morning was bright and sunny in Bonaventure. Azellia met Magnolia at the plantation. They would go to the bank together to make their presentation. Magnolia spoke with her mother about their plans, and Amellia was pleased. She was up having tea and feeling better than she had in weeks. Since Camellia was also present to wish her sisters luck at the bank, Amellia prayed with her girls and asked God to protect them and give them insight to help them be successful in their endeavors. She kissed each of their hands as she would every night before bed. She assured them that God would be present and have the last say. And as expected, she reminded them once again of their traditional saying that she had taught them when they were little girls, *"If it is to be, it shall be; show us so that we can see."*

Downstairs, Camellia hugged her sisters as they departed for the bank. She reinforced their family prayer by whispering it once more in their ears as they left, "Remember, dear sisters, *"If it is to be, it shall be."* They left feeling empowered and anxious at the same time. Even though all three sisters knew the power of their prayers, Camellia stood the strongest in the belief. Prayer and meditation were a large part of her spirituality, and she practiced them often. However, after meeting with their mother and knowing they had Camellia's blessing, Azellia and Magnolia both had a sense of calmness and assurance.

The drive to the bank seemed like an eternity, although it was only forty-five minutes away. They both found themselves repeating their chant and singing, "Lord, your will be done." They were early for their meeting.

Magnolia held Azellia's hand, looked her in the eye, and said, "Sister, it is already done. Be calm and confident. Keep your spirit peaceful. Validate what we already know, for it will be done."

The bank's president, Mr. Duparc, was very familiar with the Devereaux sisters and a longtime family friend. He welcomed them to his office. Azellia began her magic, laying out the financials. She explained that with the improvements planned, the plantation would be worth three times as much. They would be able to repay the loan in three years. Mr. Duparc was very impressed and, without hesitation, agreed to the terms. The sisters shook hands and thanked Mr. Duparc for having confidence in them. Now excited and knowing they had succeeded, they were off to the work at hand!

The sisters' plan was working out well. It had been ninety days, and the improvements were successfully taking place. The air seemed different. The trees seemed to sway in unison, and the sweet smell of lavender filled the entire pathway leading up to the Devereaux's main house. Azellia stopped by to have morning tea with her mother. It was Thursday, which was her day to spend time with her. The housekeeper, Miss Carrie, informed her that Ameliia was not feeling well and refused to eat. Azellia said she would take her tea upstairs and try to get her to eat later. As she walked up the stairs, she could smell the sweet scent of sandalwood and sage, her mother's favorite. Amellia would always say that sage and sandalwood were very calming and purifying. It helped clear your thoughts and provided positive energy for clarity and discernment.

But as she approached the landing, Azellia became overwhelmed with a feeling of utter sadness and loss. Her spirit felt broken. In her heart, she already knew that her mother had transitioned to her heavenly home. As she entered her mother's suite, Azellia's shaky voice called out to her, "Mommy, I have your tea. Won't you enjoy a cup with me?" When she did not hear her mother's response, "A cup of tea just for you and me?" she knew.

Azellia instructed Miss Carrie to phone the sisters and get them to the house. She sat with her mother and began singing "Blessed Assurance" until the sisters arrived. She felt the warmth of her mother's spirit and knew that singing her favorite song would give her peace and reassurance that the girls would be okay and would do what was best for the business. When Magnolia and Camellia arrived, Azellia had already prepared their mother's suite for prayer and meditation. They hugged each other and surrounded Amellia's bed. As they joined Azellia in song, Magnolia had a strange feeling sweep over her. She told the sisters that they were about to enter a new season, unlike anything they had experienced before, and would need strength to help them through it. They lit their candles one by one. Camellia prayed for strength, Magnolia prayed for direction, and Azellia prayed for discernment. They all prayed for unity. Then, they each took a piece of Amellia's jewelry and one of her fine lace handkerchiefs, blew out the candles, and went downstairs to call the mortuary.

Bonaventure mourned the passing of Amellia Devereaux in grand style. Every businessman and businesswoman from 100 miles east to west attended the celebration. Miss Amellia was a beloved member of Macedonia Baptist Church, where she blessed the congregation with her angelic voice for many years. Its members filled the church to capacity. Everyone wanted to say their final goodbyes to this woman of such high esteem. After the regalia was over and the sisters were alone, they wept, prayed, and sang for the acceptance of their mother's spirit into heaven's gates. They each took another of her possessions and locked her room for clearing and cleansing.

CHAPTER 3

"TIME"

Almost two years had gone by since Amellia's passing. The plantation's improvements had proven successful, and business was running favorably. The sisters were all still adjusting to their mother being gone, each trying to be preoccupied with something or someone. Magnolia had begun studying the piano again. She played beautifully but had little time of late to really pursue it due to the expansion of the plantation. Camellia decided to accept the Assistant Dean's position at the school. Having worked there for so long, she knew she would be able to make a change there, and this was her chance to do so. Meanwhile, Azellia was constantly grinding, positioning Devereaux Plantation to be one of the state's most lucrative businesses. Although, there seemed to be another slight distraction for her.

Magnolia confided in Camellia that something was "happening" with Azellia. Time would reveal it, but Magnolia had an uneasy feeling about what that would be. Azellia was very secretive. You would only know if something was going on if and when she wanted you to know. And Magnolia believed that there was. After all, she would often say, "Washington, DC changed Zell, and I'm not sure it was for the better."

It was time for the sisters' yearly meeting with the bank. They were in their second year of the loan and were excited to see the plantation's progress. Magnolia and Camellia met Azellia at Mr. Duparc's office. He was happy to see the Devereaux sisters and told them he was sorry about Amellia. Mr. Duparc said this every time they saw him and made it seem as if Amelia had just passed away, even though it had been nearly two years. He expressed his loyalty and gratitude to the Devereauxs since they were among the bank's longest and most loyal customers.

As they sat down to meet and review the plantation's progress, Mr. Duparc asked if they minded if he had one of his senior officers join them for the meeting. He explained that this individual was new to the bank and he would be managing the Devereaux account. He wanted the sisters to become acquainted with him. They agreed to meet him. When the new senior officer walked into the office, he immediately smiled and spoke to Azellia. She was shocked and delighted at the same time.

"Why hello, Mr. Guidry. I didn't know you worked at this particular bank," she exclaimed.

The sisters were stunned. They looked at Azellia with wonder in their eyes. She immediately introduced them and explained that she had met Francois Guidry about six months ago at a conference in Atlanta. He was a handsome man who favored a young Duke Ellington. He was tall and slender with light brown eyes and wavy hair. He had a small mole by his left nostril and was definitely a head-turner! The sisters, however, were looking at Azellia with the side eye. Magnolia thought to herself, *Six months ago, my ass!* That explained her feeling that something was "going on" with Azellia. Now she knew the "preoccupation" had a face and a name, and he was their new account manager. Was this a coincidence or fate?

Camellia was also full of questions about Francois Guidry. *How did Zell meet him? Was he from Bonaventure? Who was his family?* But like Magnolia, she remained as quiet as a church mouse. Azellia, on the other hand, could feel the vibe loud and clear.

The Devereaux sisters had never married. There were rumors that Magnolia was engaged to a man who turned out to be a scoundrel of the worst kind, who somehow or another left town without even a goodbye. Magnolia never saw or heard of him again. Rumors were that Amellia had "taken care" of him for humiliating and disgracing her daughter. Camellia was devoted to her students and teaching. She never had time for any type of meaningful relationship. Camellia had long ago put the thought of marriage out of her head. Teaching and her students were her life, and she was 150% devoted to that. At the same time, Azellia was too ambitious to have a relationship at this point in her life. She was turning thirty-six and her focus was on getting the plantation ready to sell, not on a man or relationships. Or so the sisters thought. But only time would truly tell since things seemed uncertain at the moment.

Two months passed, and not a word was spoken about Francois Guidry. Magnolia was so outdone by the fact that

Azellia knew him and never talked about him to the sisters. She felt betrayed and believed that Azellia intentionally kept their acquaintance a secret. Meanwhile, Camellia, who was once again in the middle, decided she had about enough of this foolishness between Magnolia and Azellia and called a family meeting. Both of them were shocked and intrigued because Camellia NEVER called any meetings unless it was related to her students. *What was up with Mell, and why was she being so direct with the sisters?*

When Magnolia and Azellia arrived, Camellia escorted them into the family parlor. Since Amellia's passing, the sisters agreed that Camellia would move back to their family home at Devereaux Plantation. It was essential to maintain a human presence until they were ready to sell. Someone would still need to watch over the caretakers, who would remain as their employees. As they entered the parlor, they could smell their mother's favorite scent of sandalwood and sage. Camellia offered them tea, and they sat around the table and prayed.

Camellia began the conversation by asking Azellia why they didn't know about Francois Guidry. She admitted that she and Magnolia were a little unsettled about the fact that Azellia knew him and did not bother to tell them. More importantly, Camellia told them both that this "feud" was getting ridiculous. Barely speaking for months, Azellia hardly ever came to the house anymore, and it was getting to be way too much for Camellia's heart to handle. They never had Saturday tea down by the water's edge together anymore. They never had Sunday dinner in the backyard anymore. And they NEVER attended church together. Camellia began to cry. She asked Azellia what was going on and WHY she was so secretive.

Magnolia raised her eyebrow and folded her arms, staring directly at Amellia's portrait. "Seems to me secrets have overtaken the good sense of some of us," she stated in her firm, matter-of-fact voice. "There is one thing we promised to never do, and that was to keep secrets from each other. But Miss Azellia doesn't seem to abide by any of our rules anymore. I guess we're too backwards thinking for her now."

Azellia immediately became defensive. "I'm thirty-six years old. I do not have to tell y'all anything about what I do. Mell, did you tell us that you turned down the Assistant Dean's position at your beloved school? No, you did not."

Magnolia immediately came to Camellia's defense, "She told me."

Camellia stuttered but managed to say, "Zell, you're never around us. It's like you have another family, and you only communicate with any of us if there is a business concern that requires our input. I always feel like I'm bothering you, so I just limited my contact to give you the space you seem to want."

Azellia could not believe what she was hearing. She could not believe she had alienated the one person she could always count on. She just instantly blamed Magnolia for influencing Camellia and swaying her to her side. "I never wanted to have this distance between us," she exclaimed. "I never thought knowing Francois would lead to a rift between you and me, Mell. I didn't think it would threaten our family's relationship and sisterly bond." She shouted, "It was just an honest coincidence! I did not know he worked for our bank!"

Still angry, she continued to rant on and on for at least fifteen minutes until she was exhausted from the conversation. She finally said, "Look, I'm sorry for any hard feelings or feelings of mistrust. I honestly did not know. I miss y'all. I need my big sisters." Camellia hugged her and told her they missed her too and just wanted things to be normal again.

It was apparent that Magnolia was softened by Azellia's "speech" as well. When she was done, Magnolia explained, "It was just bizarre that we went to the bank for a meeting, and our new account manager was someone you had met, what, six months ago? It did not feel coincidental."

Azellia assured them that she was just as shocked as they were. She knew he worked at a bank. But she assumed it was in Atlanta, not their bank in Bonaventure. After continuing to talk for about two hours or so, Camellia said she believed Azellia and was ready to move forward. Magnolia was still reluctant, but she agreed. But, she told Azellia that if she and Mr. Guidry started something other than a business relationship, they would have to have a discussion about that. She also told her she understood that she was grown. However, since her actions could have possible effects on the family business, it was something that the sisters needed to discuss to avoid any misunderstandings.

In the meantime, the plantation was doing very well. The new systems were working, and Azellia's plan proved to be just what the plantation needed. They even had an offer from the largest corn conglomerate in St. Charles Parish. It was exactly what the sisters had hoped for, and Azellia happily presented it to them.

However, Magnolia shocked them both by saying, "No. We're not selling. As I recall, and I'm sure Mell remembers, we agreed to wait until the fourth year and then, we would sell. Was this not the plan, Zell? Why the rush to sell now?"

Camellia was silent. Azellia argued, "Now is a perfect time to sell. Francois has shown me the financials and they are way ahead of their projected profits."

Whoa!!!! Magnolia was hot! She reminded Azellia that the agreement was that she and Mr. Guidry would never discuss their family business unless all three sisters were present. "So, when did you and Mr. Guidry review the financials, Zell?"

Azellia knew she had overspoken and had to fess up and be truthful with her sisters. "We went to a concert together, and afterward, we had coffee. The next day, I stopped by the bank to take care of some business for the LeBlanc family. They are one of my biggest clients, and Francois asked me if I had a minute to chat. It was totally innocent, Maggie." She finished by saying they could sell now, split their fortune, and move on with their lives.

Magnolia stared at her mother's portrait for what seemed like an eternity. She looked at Azellia with fire in her eyes, and her final answer was, "No." Magnolia got her coat and purse, marched out of the house, and never looked back. *We are not selling right now.* The more Magnolia thought about it driving home, the more she began to have second thoughts about even selling at all. After all, it was her father's wish to never sell unless it was to another Devereaux.

CHAPTER 4

"MUD"

Months had passed since Magnolia and Azellia had spoken. The sisters were feuding, and Camellia was smack in the middle. She absolutely hated it! They would talk through Camellia but never to each other. There were no phone calls or visits to the family house. If Azellia were there, Magnolia would not come. If Magnolia were there, Azellia would keep going and call Camellia later. It was a mess, and Camellia was becoming depressed since they had always been as thick as thieves. She said they just all needed to be together at the family house. They needed to absorb positive energy. Negative energy was abundant, and they needed to mitigate it.

Camellia lit her candles and burned sage. She prayed for goodness and solidarity. As always, she ended her prayer with, *"If it is to be, it shall be, show us so that we can see."*

Although the Devereaux sisters were at odds, Azellia was living her life. Her relationship with Francois Guidry blossomed, and the parish folks could hear wedding bells. Talk around town was that Azellia had a new beau and that things were pretty serious for the Devereaux's baby girl.

After long thought and meditation, Camellia confronted Azellia about the talk of the town. Azellia admitted the relationship had gone to another level, and she was thrilled. She also told Camellia to tell "her" sister Magnolia that Francois had already been removed from their account, and if she had been at the meeting two months ago, she would have known that. So, there was no reason why she and Francois could not build on their relationship and even get married if they chose to.

Needless to say, Camellia was shocked and completely speechless. Once she regained her composure, she told Azellia she wasn't upset but happy she found love and happiness. Camellia confessed that she and Magnolia were set in their ways but that she would convince Magnolia to accept the situation and move forward. Camellia knew Magnolia would be hurt, but she would eventually come to peace with it. She suggested that Francois come to dinner so everyone could be properly introduced. Azellia agreed and told Camellia to break the news to Magnolia. Azellia didn't want any surprises or shenanigans, and she really wanted them to get to know Francois.

On Thursday night, Azellia and Francois were prompt for their dinner engagement with the other sisters. The house smelled of all of Azellia's favorite foods, especially her mother's gumbo and fried green tomatoes. Camellia was a great cook, and she loved being in the kitchen with her mother when she was a young girl, learning all of the family's secret recipes and making some of their own. She had created a heavenly meal for them to enjoy, and hopefully, it would soften Magnolia's heart towards Azellia and Francois' relationship. Camellia even prepared Magnolia's favorite bread pudding with a special Grand Marnier cream sauce. She brought out the "big dogs" for this. She mused, *If I ever got a husband, one thing for sure is that his entire soul would be deliciously fed!*

After Azellia and Francois arrived, Magnolia offered everyone a little "before dinner" drink to break the ice and get everyone in a more relaxed state of mind. Before she could finish pouring her drink, Camellia asked Francois, "Mr. Guidry, where are you from and do you have family here?" Magnolia smirked as she took her seat right by her mother's portrait and waited for his response.

"Well, my mother is from around Cheneaux," he answered. "She lived there when she was a child. She had two sisters: Naomi, who was four years older than she was, and BethMae, who was ten years older. They had the same father, but not the same mother. I believe their last name was Boudreaux. My mother always talks about her sisters. She always talks about playing with Naomi on their grandfather's farm. BethMae never came around much. She has no idea where they are or if they would even remember her. She suspects her older sister might be deceased, but she was not sure about Naomi. My mother said her family left the area when she was about ten years old. They later moved to Baton Rouge when she was about fourteen or fifteen, and she lived there until my father passed three years ago. She moved to Texas, where her best friend from college lives. I talk to her at least once a week. She's happy, so I'm happy. I have one sister, Lilian, who's a dance instructor and lives in Chicago. That's about it. I came back to Baton Rouge for career advancement. When my mother decided to move to Texas, I came here because I was offered a position at the bank that I could not turn down. The bank president met all of my requests so this will be my home," he concluded while winking at Azellia.

His response seemed to satisfy the sisters, even Magnolia. She started opening up more and being more receptive, even inviting him to church.

Time grew, and things progressed with Azellia and Francois. Magnolia warmed up a little more, but still maintained a certain distance. They had one year left with the bank. The plantation was thriving. Everything was going well. Magnolia had even been talking with Azellia and was very cordial, yet cautious. Something still was not quite right, but she could not put her finger on it. Magnolia knew something was in the air when Azellia asked if they could all meet at the house. She needed to discuss a proposition with them. With curiosity piqued, the sisters agreed to meet with Azellia.

CHAPTER 5

"COMPROMISE"

Camellia had the entire house redecorated to fit her taste. It was serene, calm, and very zen. She donated everything she didn't want to the local shelters and churches. Camellia was a compassionate soul who only always wanted to do the right thing. Magnolia, on the other hand, had become hard with little compassion. She was all about the business.

Azellia was fifteen minutes late to their meeting, and you can best believe Magnolia made sure to point it out every five minutes. Camellia saw Azellia pull in front, and she told Magnolia, "She's here."

Magnolia proceeded to go into the sitting room. The sisters started every meeting as they always did with candles and prayer and were extremely meticulous in what they prayed for. Their mother taught them to always pray with intent and purpose and to remember what she taught them when they were young. As

31

her grandmother had taught her, *"If it is to be, it shall be, show us so that we can see."* She would always say there was great power in those words as long as you trusted them and believed.

After they finished praying, Camellia offered tea and beignets. Azellia was eager to speak. "Sisters, I have given long and deep thought to this. I don't have to pretend. Talk is almost literally walking the streets of Bonaventure with speculation of Francois' and my relationship."

Magnolia sipped her tea and acknowledged what Azelia was saying. Camellia just listened. Azellia continued, "Y'all know I want to sell. It's apparent y'all don't, so my compromise is that y'all buy me out. That way we sorta honor both our parents' wishes and we can all get what we want."

Magnolia continued to sip her tea. Camellia thought for a minute and then said, "Zell, if that will make you happy and bring us back together again as a family, I'm all for it. I believe it is a good compromise. Maggie, what about you?"

Magnolia sat her teacup down, straightened her glasses, and said, "How much?"

Azellia was shocked! She was all ready to plead her case. She had practiced her comebacks to Magnolia's resistance. Azellia was speechless. Camellia's eyes were as wide as a rabbit's. She, too, was shocked. Azellia collected her thoughts and said, "Well, three-way split. Ya'll give me my third in cash, and we have a deal. No fuss, no muss. Is that fair Maggie?"

Now, instead of agreeing with what was a fair compromise, Magnolia looked at Camellia, not Azellia, and said, "Let me look at our financials and discuss it with Mell and of course, our financial advisor. I want to make sure we all get what's rightfully ours. Give us a week, and we'll let you know."

Flabbergasted, Azellia just nodded her head yes, gathered her things, and left. Once she saw Azellia drive off, Camellia asked Magnolia what that was all about. *Zell's offer was fair. A three-way split,* she thought to herself. *That's how it should be. So what was there to think about?* Magnolia, however, looked Camellia dead in the eye and said, "I am the CEO of the Devereaux Plantation and I will decide what is fair."

Camellia nodded, picked up the tea cups, and left Magnolia standing there with her hands on her hips while staring at Amellia's portrait. There would be no more discussion on that subject, and Camellia knew when to let well enough alone. She silently mumbled, *"If it is to be, it shall be, show us so that we can see."*

After almost two weeks, Magnolia called her sisters and arranged a meeting at the house. Camellia was nervous because she hadn't spoken to Magnolia in a week or so. When Magnolia arrived, she told Camellia that no discussion was needed unless she had something relevant to say. Camellia said, "All I want is for us to be a family, for whatever that means. You are the oldest, Maggie. I trust your judgment. I just ask that you be kind and compassionate in your decision. And that it be without judgment, or spite, or anything of that sort. I ask that you allow Zell to be happy and live her life with someone who loves her, regardless of whatever that means for us. I just want our family back together. That's it, Maggie. That's it," she sighed. After a few moments, she heard Azellia walking towards them. "She's here."

Azellia came in with hugs and what appeared to be small gifts. Each gift was wrapped in their favorite colors. She gave Magnolia the red one and Camellia the yellow one. The sisters prayed and meditated before their meeting. Camellia prayed for guidance, compassion, and peace. She offered tea to the sisters. Azellia began by asking them to look in their bags. She had collected special items with special meanings for each of them.

She could see Magnolia soften just a little bit. "Why Zell, what a thoughtful and sweet gift. I don't know what to say," she exclaimed as she looked lovingly at the beautiful hair comb. The lace was exquisite, and Magnolia loved it.

Camellia burst out, "Thank you will be fine, Sister, just say thank you." They hugged and laughed, something they had not done together in at least two years. Magnolia replaced her braided comb with the beautiful laced one. She absolutely loved it. Camellia looked up at their mother's portrait and whispered a soft "thank you," for she knew her prayers had been answered.

Magnolia sat down first. She requested that Azellia sit next to her. Azellia sat next to Magnolia and looked at her with wonder. "Sister, I was hoping for a peaceful reconciliation," Azellia said in a soft and humble voice. "This thing between us, this feud, has weighed heavily on me and has gone on far too long. I just want to be happy."

Camellia was almost in tears but took a deep breath so she wouldn't start crying because she knew she had to show strength at this very moment. Magnolia took Azellia's hands and said, "I have been unreasonable, little chicken, and I apologize," she replied, calling her by the name she had used when they were younger and were making up after a fight. "I was just so upset about you wanting to sell so quickly and not adhering to our original plan. You know I am all about staying on course. I just overreacted and let things get way out of hand. You presented a fair compromise."

Azellia smiled and pushed Magnolia's hair out of her face. "Sister, I would never do anything to hurt y'all, you know that. I felt like you did not want me to be happy simply because you CHOSE not to be happy." Azellia knew she had struck a chord with Magnolia and anticipated a backlash.

Magnolia looked at her and said, "You are absolutely right."

Camellia looked at Magnolia, thinking, *OK, she must have put brandy in that tea.* But Magnolia simply stood up and went to her purse. She took out an envelope and gave it to Azellia. As Azellia began to open the envelope, Magnolia said, "We'll agree to the buyout, and our terms are stated in the paperwork in the envelope. If that will make you happy, we'll proceed. Mell is right. This feud between us has gone on far too long. It is time for the Devereaux sisters to reunite and bring love back into this beautiful old house."

Azellia was so happy. She said she would get the bank to draw up the papers as stated in Magnolia and Camellia's agreement. They would settle the financial matters, and they could all move forward. She hugged her sisters and thanked them for understanding and allowing her some happiness. Camellia and Magnolia watched as their baby sister got in her car and drove away, literally on cloud nine. She could go and live her life with the man she loved, with no faults and no regrets. She had the love and support of her sisters and her share of the Devereaux fortune. It was a grand day indeed.

CHAPTER 6

"AGREEMENT"

Azellia was planning her wedding. The sisters were excited and offered to help in any way. Magnolia, of course, wanted to take charge. She told Azellia that since their parents were both gone, it was her duty to give her the most fabulous wedding Bonaventure had ever seen. Camellia was so excited. This was the first wedding in their family since their parents' wedding and maybe the first of more to come. Camellia loved weddings, decorating, and making things look beautiful. She located a wedding designer and coordinator in nearby Hammond. Magnolia agreed that Camellia could handle that part and work with the designer to ensure Azellia had exactly what she wanted. Magnolia would handle the caterer and the guest list. They were all set!

The town was abuzz with the Devereaux sisters and Azellia's wedding. Everyone loved the Devereaux family. Vacherre and

Amellia were beloved by all in Bonaventure, so naturally, their girls were also recipients of that same love. There were many parties and events celebrating Azellia and her fiance. From her sorority sisters, the friends she made at Howard University, and her church family, gifts came in from all over Virginia, California, DC, and everywhere in between. Folks were showering Azellia and Francois with love.

It was three months before the big day. Azellia had to go out of town for an important meeting. Francois could not accompany her due to work obligations. Magnolia assured Azellia that they would take good care of him and make sure he ate properly. Magnolia and Camellia had a plan and had to execute it before Azellia returned, so the timing was perfect!

Azellia returned home after three days of tough negotiations but with a favorable outcome for her client. She was excited to tell Francois about her trip. But, when she arrived home, there was a note to meet him at the Devereaux house. Azellia hurried to her car and headed for their family home. She thought, *What is going on now? I know everything is going great with the business, so what could be so important to summon us to Devereaux House?* Azellia was contemplating a gazillion scenarios in her mind. She hadn't a clue. She drove near the lavender-laced driveway, thinking, *What does Maggie have up her sleeve?* When she entered the parlor, everyone was waiting for her.

The sisters did not go through their usual family meeting ritual. With Francois there, they felt it wasn't appropriate. Besides, this was a joyful occasion, and nothing more was needed to make it great. Magnolia offered champagne to everyone. However, while excited, she and Camellia also seemed anxious to say whatever it was that summoned Azellia and Francois to the house.

Magnolia took out a large white envelope with Azellia's name on it. She handed it to her and then took her seat by the piano. As Azellia began to open the envelope, Magnolia and Camellia smiled at each other with delight. "What is this, Maggie?" she asked suspiciously.

"Exactly what it says, Zell," Magnolia stated firmly. Azellia was shocked. Camellia, being such a soft-hearted individual, began to cry. Azellia handed the contents of the envelope to Francois.

Francois was concerned at first until he began reading the document. "Magnolia, are you sure? Are you sure?"

Magnolia stood up and faced her mother's portrait. "We've decided not to buy you out, Zell. It just did not sit well in my spirit, nor Mell's. What we would like to propose is this: you will become the head of the Devereaux Plantation's legal department, with a grand salary, of course. You will no longer have the shared responsibility of ownership of the Devereaux Plantation, nor will you sit on the board. Still, you will have voting privileges for major decisions. If you accept our proposal, you will become head counsel, along with a whole other set of important responsibilities. Camellia and I thought it over and we thought this was the best thing for all of us."

Azellia was in shock but managed to speak with gratitude and happiness in her voice. "My sisters, I am overwhelmed. I did not expect such a generous offer." Tears welled up in her eyes, and her voice was shaky as she spoke. "I am grateful, and I promise you both I will give you one hundred percent. Thank y'all, from the bottom of my heart! Thank y'all so very much." It was actually a perfect plan. She would be free of the bulk of responsibility and could focus on her new life with Francois and everything that would bring her joy. She was happy and told her sisters that the storm was seeming to cease, with joy and brighter days ahead. Camellia started praying with the sisters, and Francois joined in. They were once again a family, which is what Camellia had prayed for.

The Devereaux House seemed to shine with a newfound brightness. Both Vacherre and Amellia could rest in peace knowing that their children had reunited and all their issues seemed to be solved. Peace had been restored.

CHAPTER 7

"BUSINESS"

The wedding day was nearing. Magnolia called a family meeting. She instructed Azellia to make sure Francois was in attendance. As CEO and President of Devereaux Corporation, she had important business matters that needed to be settled before the wedding, and she knew it was up to her to get things moving. When Azellia and Francois arrived, Miss Carrie led them to the study and not to the parlor this time, which seemed a little bizarre to Azellia. Unexpectedly, Schaffer Comier, an attorney on staff at Devereaux Corporation, was in the study. Schaffer was a petite young woman with a short, curly pixie haircut. She was a product of an interracial marriage, but her features were predominately caucasian. However, her personality was one hundred percent Black. She graduated at the top of her class from Southern University Law School and moved back to Bonaventure to be near her parents. Schaffer Comier was definitely someone you would want on your legal team. Very ambitious and very knowledgeable, she was definitely an asset to the Devereaux Corporation. Azellia looked at Magnolia and Camellia with wonder and asked, "What's going on, Maggie?"

"Well, since you have been so busy with the wedding, I thought we should go ahead and get the prenuptial agreement settled and out of the way."

"Huh," stuttered Azellia. She was shocked and more than a little bit angry. "Oh, you think we need a prenuptial agreement? Why would you think that and then just go behind my back to have it arranged? Really, Maggie!"

Ms. Comier interjected with sound information, trying to calm things down before Azellia lost it. "Azellia, it is a natural expectation to have a prenuptial agreement when such a large fortune is involved. I do not have to tell you the value of the entire Devereaux Corporation, nor do I need to break down any numbers for you. With that being said, it is very important to have a prenuptial agreement in place to protect the family assets. You of all people know that."

Azellia was still looking very bewildered. She did know that, but she was still angry. "Maggie, why are you doing this?"

Magnolia firmly stated that she was doing it to protect the family and everything their father and mother had worked all their lives to obtain. She told Francois that it was nothing personal. It was strictly a business move, and she truly hoped he understood. But from his demeanor, it appeared that Francois had "zoned out" and was oblivious to what was being discussed. "Francois, excuse me, did you hear what we said?" she asked.

Francois looked at Azellia and said, "Yes, I get it and I understand. Honestly, I expected Azellia to say something about this, but since she had not, I figured she didn't care about it. I understand the financial implications of the prenuptial agreement, and I have no objections to it. I guess I'm just shocked that Magnolia did it and did not tell you, Azellia. I want to be sure that we are all clear on this - I make my own living and I do not intend to live off of my wife and her family. I have made good, sound business decisions and I have invested well with what my father left me as an inheritance. So, I can take care of Azellia," he emphasized. Francois signed the agreement and assured the sisters of his love for Azellia and his ability to care for her properly.

Magnolia expressed her pleasure with the situation and thanked Francois for being so straightforward. She told him she could respect a man who was honest, and she trusted his word unless he would give her a reason not to. Azellia and Francois could live their lives however they chose to, and Magnolia had peace of mind knowing that the Devereaux fortune was bound and protected, no matter what the future held. As far as she was concerned, everything was good with the Devereauxs.

But Amellia's face was still red as beets, and she was steaming! "Maggie, I am so upset with you right now! How could you do this behind my back? You know nothing about Francois and his ability to take care of me." Francois tried to calm Azellia down, reassuring her that he was in agreement with the prenup. He told her it was the right thing to do business-wise, and he understood the need for it.

Magnolia, staring at their mother's portrait, spoke to Azellia in her stern voice. "Zell, I felt I needed to take care of business. And this was strictly business. I am sorry if you feel a certain way, but I did what I felt was best, and Camellia agreed with me. If you could take care of this, it would be one less thing for you and Francois to be bothered with. You can be upset, and that's okay. But as I said, this is business, and as CEO, I felt it was my business to make sure it was done."

Azellia looked at Francois, and he nodded, reaffirming that he was good. Azellia looked at Magnolia and, calming down, said, "I appreciate your concern, and I do realize that you did this out of love for me and our parents' company. I do understand that. However, it would have been less of an ordeal had you just come to me and said you were doing it. I think I would have accepted it better."

To everyone's astonishment, Magnolia stated, "You are right. I probably should have. But you know how I am."

Camellia laughed and said, "Oh yes, Sister, we all know how you are." That brought a chuckle even to Azellia.

"I will try to mind only Devereaux family business from here on out, but I can't make any promises." Magnolia smiled and winked at Francois. Tensions eased, and all had been forgiven. Azellia resolved that Magnolia is who she is and that she would always be Magnolia!

PART TWO

PART TWO

CHAPTER 8

"CURIOSITY"

Francois and Azellia were going to the airport in Baton Rouge to pick up Francois' mother, Katherine Guidry. Mrs. Guidry was a beautiful woman who had aged very well. Her skin was flawless, and no one would ever believe she was eighty-four years old. Her hair was silvery colored, short, and curly, matching her sassy personality. You knew she was from the old school of "good hair and good color," and her persona reflected that.

After picking her up, their first stop was at the Devereaux Plantation to introduce Mrs. Guidry to the sisters. As they drove down the lavender-lined driveway, she admired the grounds and the beautiful flowers in bloom. "This reminds me of my grandfather's home in Cheneaux. He was white you know, but he was a good grandfather and he surely loved us all. I had two sisters. I remember them, but I was young when we moved away. They could be dead," she said sadly.

"I know that my dad once said that they were somewhere down South, maybe in Mississippi, or maybe even still in Louisiana, but I honestly do not have a clue. My oldest sister was named Bethel, but we called her BethMae. And my other sister was named Naomi. We had the same father, but not the same mother. Even though she was older than me, folks used to say that Naomi and I looked like twins. Bethel looked like her mother. She was a little darker, but she had our dad's features. Especially his eyes. I do not recall their mother's last name. We shared our father's last name of Boudreaux. I would suspect that BethMae has long passed away. She would be almost ninety-five years old if she were still alive. Naomi should be about eighty-eight, I think. I'm sure she married," she said mournfully, then continued. "She was a beautiful girl. I haven't a clue what her name would be or where she would be. I have always had faith that one day we will be reunited. But nevertheless, not knowing anything about her, it saddens my soul."

"Mother, I am still searching," Francois interjected. "I am still searching, and I promise you I will find your siblings. As soon as we're settled with the wedding stuff, I will vigorously resume my search, Cher. I promise. You mustn't give up hope and you must remain faithful. I promise you, Cher." That brought a smile to Katherine's face.

As they pulled into the main driveway, Magnolia was on the porch waiting for them to arrive. She met them at the car and welcomed Mrs. Guidry to the Devereaux's house. "We are so pleased to meet you, Ma'am. Welcome to our home and to our family. We are looking forward to what the future will bring," she exclaimed. "Francois, your mother is lovely!"

Katherine hugged Magnolia and Camellia. She, too, was delighted to meet them. They proceeded into the parlor for refreshments before dinner. Katherine admired the portrait of Amellia. "What a stunning woman. Your mother?"

Camellia replied, "Yes, Ma'am, our beloved mother Amellia. She transitioned almost six years ago. Her spirit lives on here with us, in this glorious place."

Very curiously, Katherine asked, "Was she Creole?"

Magnolia looked stunned but composed herself and answered, "Her mother, our grandmother, was French. Mother looked very much like her, except her eyes were hazel, and as you can see, our mother's eyes were a deep, dark brown. Our mother was a very beautiful and mysterious woman, with many special gifts. Her faith in God and His universe was unshakeable. She studied the signs and she was very spiritual." *Creole? What difference does it make if she was or wasn't Creole?* It just hit Magnolia's spirit wrong.

Camellia looked at Magnolia like she had said something sinister and as if she wanted to see how Mrs. Guidry would respond. "Shall we have another drink before dinner?" Camellia insisted, trying to lighten the mood.

Francois and Azellia were already on their second drink, neither saying a word after Magnolia's bizarre comments. Magnolia, with her famous smirk, simply sipped her drink while winking at Camellia, just for grins! Magnolia and Camellia found humor in the conversation with Mrs. Guidry, even though they were not sure Francois and Azellia did. But the drinks certainly helped!

After a delicious meal, they sat out on the porch and admired the beautiful grounds, which were in full bloom. The air was crisp and smelled of lavender and magnolias. Camellia asked Katherine how long she would be staying. Katherine told the sisters that she had planned to stay awhile and return back to Texas in a few months. She said she was going to do some research of her own while she was down South to try to locate her siblings. Magnolia told Katherine she could stay at Devereaux House, and Camellia agreed. She told Katherine they would help her with her search and prayed that she found them. Family was important, and Naomi was most likely Katherine's only living sibling. It was paramount that they find her and reunite them before time slipped away from both of them.

CHAPTER 9

"BEGINNINGS"

The wedding was beautiful. The guests were the "who's who" of Bonaventure and beyond. Azellia was the most beautiful bride ever, and Francois was quite the dapper groom. Her dress was a custom gown from the House of Claire, the most exquisite bridal salon in Bonaventure. It was very ornate and covered with pearls and sequins. It had long, intricately designed sleeves attached to a fitted bodice embellished in lace. Its regal train was made of chiffon, and the veil was cathedral length, with miniature lavender roses enfolding the edge. It was simple yet elegant and timeless. She felt gorgeous and captured the attention of every guest as she made her way down the courtyard's pathway to her groom, who was waiting for her at the end of the beautifully decorated garden.

Camellia had outdone herself with the decor. Flowers were everywhere, and the sweet smell of lavender engulfed the grounds.

The tables were magnificently dressed with china, crystal, and memorabilia of the bride's and groom's childhoods. Of course, the food was delicious and catered by the LaSalle Family. They were the best Southern caterers this side of the Mississippi and served the finest cuisine. Their specialty was prime rib with a delectable cognac sauce. Azellia's favorite was the dirty rice, so there was plenty to go around.

The wedding cake was very traditional, with five tiers and a champagne fountain running from both sides. The delicate lavender roses that adorned the entire cake made it look like a work of art. Inside, of course, was Azellia's favorite red velvet cake that literally melted in your mouth. It was truly spectacular! The guests all made comments about how beautiful everything was. Camellia truly had her mother's gift for extraordinarily beautiful designs and decor, and it showed in every aspect of the event. Folks were dancing, eating, and enjoying one of the community's most festive celebrations.

Azellia and Francois left shortly after the reception for an extended honeymoon in Greece. They were looking forward to just letting their hair down and taking a long-needed rest. Things would be moving fast once they got back home, so relaxation was paramount for the Guidrys. Upon their return, the first thing Azellia needed to do was hire a legal intern to help her with her new responsibilities. She was hoping to find a recent graduate who was fresh and eager. In the meantime, she meditated and prayed for the right one to come along.

The newlyweds had a fantastic time and were able to really enjoy each other away from the day-to-day stressors of work. However, Magnolia and Camellia were excited to see Azellia and Francois return from Greece. Mrs. Guidry was still there and helped Camellia prepare a wonderful dinner for them. There were greens, mac and cheese, yams, baked ham, and, of course, dirty rice.

Azellia was relaxed but anxious to get back to it. She had five interviews set up for her intern position. They all looked good, but one stood out to her. Her only concern was he was from up north and out of state, but she was willing to interview him and see what he brought to the table. His name alone, William Thurgood Langston III, promised greatness. *Let's see if he stands up to that greatness,* Azellia thought to herself. He arrived on Thursday and would be the first applicant for her to interview. She was prepared with tough questions and scenarios to see if he was up to the challenge of being her intern.

On her first day back to the office, Azellia was up and on the phone early, getting things lined up for her day. She decided to interview only three individuals out of the five. In her mind, three interviews were sufficient to find a good intern. Two young ladies from Xavier University were on her list. She was highly impressed with one of them. Still, her field wasn't corporate law, and Azellia wanted someone with corporate law knowledge. However, she decided she would still meet with her since she had been referred to by one of Azellia's old Howard University professors. So even if it was just a "courtesy interview," she wanted to keep an open mind in case this young lady proved to be the one.

Meanwhile, Mr. Langston was fifteen minutes early for his interview. He was excited about the opportunity. Although his parents would have preferred that he stay in Boston and work with his dad at their family's firm, young Mr. Langston wanted to come to the South, where he felt he could make a difference. He also wanted to be near his grandmother and older brother in Atlanta. Being from the East Coast, the South was like an entirely different universe. He remembered coming one or two times when he was young but never really spent any quality time soaking up the Southern charm that his grandmother spoke of so frequently.

Mr. Langston was waiting for Azellia in her office. He admired her beautiful antique furniture and thought how it reminded him of his grandmother's house. The view from her office was magnificent, and he was in awe of how peaceful the surroundings made him feel. However, he came to immediate attention once Azellia entered the room. "Good morning, Mr. Langston. I see you found us without any problems. I'm Azellia Devereaux-Guidry, so nice to meet you."

"Good morning, Ma'am. It's very nice to meet you. Please, just call me Trey." Trey Langston was a handsome, mocha-colored young man. Although he was not tall in stature, it was very evident that he enjoyed spending time in the gym. He was a dread-head with light brown locs past his shoulders, which he pulled back in a ponytail. His beard made him look older but handsome nevertheless.

Azellia was impressed with Trey's confidence. When responding, he looked her dead in the eye and did not hesitate to answer any question. He had prepared to give her additional scenarios to help Azellia see the many possibilities of any situation, not just the narrow,

closed-ended version. Yes, Azellia was impressed, indeed. After interviewing the last two young ladies, it was crystal clear that Trey was the choice. He was intelligent, articulate, and confident, and he was just what Azellia and the Devereaux Corporation needed.

She discussed it with Francois and the sisters at dinner. She told them he was more than qualified, having graduated magna cum laude from the Howard University School of Law, her alma mater. She told them that he came from a family of attorneys and that his grandfather had one of the oldest black firms in Boston. The firm was very prestigious, with an impeccable reputation. Azellia told the sisters she wanted to invite Trey over to dinner, so they could meet him and feel his "spirit." That was very important to the sisters. Camellia agreed. She said she and Mrs. Guidry would put on a feast to welcome this young man to both the Devereaux Corporation and their family. Azellia was excited. She said they would invite him over in two weeks after giving him a little time to get his feet wet in his new position.

CHAPTER 10

"DISCOVERY"

Almost three weeks had passed since Trey became Devereaux's new intern, and he was progressing nicely. The morning was crisp and cool, and you could smell autumn in the air. Francois was very impressed with Tre's confidence and his knowledge of corporate law.

Azellia called Trey to her office. "Good morning Trey, hope you had a good weekend. Bonaventure is beautiful this time of the year! The trees at Devereaux House are gorgeous!"

"Good morning, Mrs. Guidry. How are you?" he responded. After she answered, he continued, "Yes, my weekend was short, but eventful. I was able to contact my brother in Atlanta and I plan to go visit sometime next month. That's the best thing about being here, I'm about three hours away from my brother and my grandmother. My grandmother moved to Atlanta last year to live with my brother and his family. Both he and his wife are self-employed and they have a teenager, and my grandmother moved to help even the playing field for my little cousin, Emerald. So, you wanted to see me Ma'am?"

"Yes, Trey. Francois and I would like for you to come to dinner so you can meet my two sisters. My sister, Magnolia, in particular. She is the president and CEO of Devereaux Plantation, and is in essence, our boss. Are you free Thursday evening?"

Trey smiled with delight. He thought to himself, *I must be doing a good job if I'm getting to meet the boss lady.* "Yes, Ma'am, I am free and I would love a good home cooked meal. Thank you for inviting me. What time should I be there?"

"How is 8:00 pm? Come around 7:30 so we can chat before sitting down for dinner.Magnolia likes to have conversation and cognac before the evening meal. Don't let her scare you. She's tough as nails, but I'm finding that in her older age, she is becoming as soft as marshmallows." That brought a laugh from both Azellia and Trey. He thanked Azellia again for the invite and told her he appreciated her kindness.

Trey called his brother, Thomi, before going to bed. He wanted to tell him how his job was going and how he was adjusting to the South and being away from home. Thomi told him that he had just talked to their mom, Carletta, and she wanted to make sure he was keeping in contact with Trey. He was happy that he could tell her that Trey would be coming to visit them, everything would be alright, and for her not to worry. Trey was glad his big brother had reassured their mom. He missed her and his dad, but he was following his own path and hoped they would understand. Trey knew he would always have the love and support of his parents. He knew he was blessed.

Katherine was up early, sitting on the porch, drinking tea and relaxing in the lovely autumn weather. Camellia called her to see if she needed a wrap. She told her no and that she was fine but wanted her to come out and join her before she left for work. Camellia enjoyed having the elder Mrs. Guidry there. She was filling a void left by Amellia, especially since she still missed her mother so much. "I will start cooking while you're at work, that way you won't have to worry about getting it all done when you get back this afternoon. Azellia said dinner at 8:00 pm, so everything will be done and ready to eat by then."

Camellia hugged Katherine before she knew it. "Ok, thank you, Mrs. Guidry! I appreciate that so much. Now, I won't have to be stressed out thinking about it at work. You are just an angel!"

"Camellia, we are family, please call me Kat. That's what my friends and family call me, so just Kat is fine."

"Ok, I will," Camellia promised. "But only if you call me Mell." She hugged her again, and it seemed tighter this time. Then she waved goodbye as she left for work.

Later on that day, Magnolia dropped by. As she entered the house, she was engulfed in the sweet aroma of fine Southern cooking. "My Lord, what are all those wonderful smells coming from this kitchen, Mrs. Guidry?

"Please call me Kat. I told Mell that we are family, and that's what my family and friends call me," she stressed. "Well, I have greens, rice dressing, mac and cheese, yams, baked ham, and fried chicken, of course. Mell is making the cornbread when she comes, and the bread pudding is almost ready for sampling, Magnolia. I hear it's your favorite," Kat said with a smile.

Magnolia thought she was home again, visiting from college, and her mom was cooking all her favorite things in the kitchen.

"Kat, you have truly outdone yourself. Between you and Mell, I'm going to be fat, full, and happy for the rest of the evening. Come and sit with me in the parlor and have a cocktail."

Kat finished up the sauce for the bread pudding and joined Magnolia in the parlor. The Devereaux House was feeling alive again. It was like the walls were singing with joy, and peace had filled the entire house.

Just as they were settling in the parlor, Camellia pulled up with Azellia and Francois. Magnolia went to greet them, and they hugged as they entered the house. The three sisters took a moment and looked at each other in utter delight. Their home smelled like old times, and they could feel the peace and rebirth of the Devereaux House. It brought joy to their hearts.

Azellia hugged Katherine and gushed, "Mother Guidry, you have been busy! The house smells wonderful!"

"You're welcome," Kat answered. "But, Mell helped too."

Camellia smiled and said, "Kat did everything but the cornbread. She even made the bread pudding for Magnolia, along with the Grand Marnier sauce that she loves so much. Give me a minute to whip up the cornbread and I'll join y'all in the parlor for drinks."

Azellia and Francois joined Magnolia and Katherine in the parlor. "Now Zell, tell me about this young man, your new intern," Magnolia said. "He seems too good to be true. I got a call from Schaffer Comier last week, praising him. And if Schaffer is giving out praises, he must be exceptional! Schaffer was very impressed with his knowledge of corporate law. She was also impressed with his passion for wanting to work with the underprivileged youth who wanted to go into their field. I told her all I knew about him was that he was from the Boston area and came from a long line of attorneys. So tell us more about this jewel, Zell."

"Well, he actually has roots here in the South, but he was born and raised near Boston. He grew up in a family of attorneys. His dad and grandfather are both attorneys and his grandfather owned one of the most prestigious law firms in Boston. His grandfather is retired, leaving Trey's father as head of the firm. Trey has a brother in Atlanta and I believe his mom's mother lives there with his brother and family. He said his grandmother was from Cheneaux, but moved when she was a young woman. She lived in Ford County until about a year or two ago when she moved to Atlanta."

Francois noticed the look on his mother's face. It looked like she was about to faint. "Mother, are you ok? Cher, what's wrong?" he asked, concern showing on his face.

Katherine looked as if she'd seen a ghost. She was speechless and almost lethargic. Just at that moment, the doorbell rang. Camellia went to answer it, and Azellia got Katherine a glass of water. Camellia ushered Trey into the parlor, and Azellia welcomed him in. "Everyone, please meet Devereaux's newest intern William Thurgood Langston III. But he goes by Trey."

After Katherine gathered herself, she thought about what she wanted to ask Trey about "who" his grandmother was. When she heard Cheneaux, her mind immediately went to her sisters. *Could this be a connection to them? How can I "break the ice" and start a conversation with him without seeming too nosey?* Nosey or not, her gut told her that this young man could be the key to locating her sisters, and she had to find out. But first, she had to calm her spirit and gather her thoughts so she could ask specific questions and maybe somehow find her sisters and be reunited with them. Her heart was pounding but full of hope.

CHAPTER 11

"REUNITED"

The evening was progressing well. Everyone was enjoying the delectable meal that Kat had prepared. As Trey was eating, he had a look of pure bliss on his face and commented on the pea salad. "Man, this reminds me of my grandmother's. She used to always say it was a family secret, but this right here reminds me of hers."

Katherine's brow peaked, "So, young man, you like my pea salad? You say your grandmother made it for you?"

"Oh yes, ma'am, my Grand-Naomi loved to cook, and pea salad was one of her favorite dishes."

Francois was sitting between his Mom and Azellia. Katherine grabbed his hand and held it tightly. "What did you call her?"

"Grand-Naomi," said Trey, "because she said she would never be called 'Granny.' Naomi is her name, actually." And just like that, Katherine knew she had found her sister!

She began to stammer, trying to get her words out. "Lord, Lord, Lord, thank you, Father! Thank you, thank you!"

Trey thought, *What in the world is going on?* "Ma'am, did I say something wrong? Are you ok?" he asked concernedly.

Katherine grabbed Trey and hugged him, almost leaving him breathless. "You have just brought unspeakable joy to me, to my life! You are telling me that YOUR grandmother is my sister Naomi Boudreaux! I haven't seen my sister Naomi since we left Chenneaux. I always wondered where they were, and if they were still alive. It's been over sixty-something years. Lord, or maybe more. I don't know, I'm just, I'm just…." Katherine began to cry and thanked the Lord for this blessing.

Everyone was shocked! Needless to say, dinner came to a halt as everyone tried to gather themselves and process what had just happened. Azellia managed to speak, "Mother Guidry, oh my God, this is wonderful news, yes? This is what you've been praying for, for years and years. God is so amazing! He created this path for all of us, and now look at this amazing situation. Trey, please can you call your grandmother?n Can you get her on the phone?" Azellia asked.

Trey was somewhat in shock himself. He could not believe that his grandmother had a sister. She never spoke of any family. He had to call his mom! "Well, I think I should call my mom or brother first. I don't want to shock Grand-Naomi. She's pretty old, you know."

Katherine snickered, "Yes, Darlin', aren't we all? Please call whomever you need to. I just can't believe this!"

Trey called home, but no one was there. He did not want to leave a message. Besides, what would he say? *Mom, I got a new job and found Grand-Naomi's sister.* No, he'd call Thomi. After about fifteen minutes on the phone with Thomi, he explained the situation and the discovery. Thomi could not believe it. No one knew about their Grand-Naomi's family. She never mentioned her family at all. Thomi was reluctant to tell her right away. He told Trey he would call him back in a few minutes. This was something he needed to tell his grandmother before letting her speak to anyone. Trey agreed.

When Trey returned to the parlor, he explained that his brother thought it best for him to break the news to their grandmother before she spoke to Katherine. Katherine was anxious, nervous, and excited, along with a gazillion other emotions going on at the same time. Meanwhile, the sisters gathered everyone together in the study to pray. They had witnessed something so miraculous and amazing! They were so happy for Katherine. Just think, Atlanta was about a three-and-a-half-hour drive. Only three and a half hours separated Katherine and Naomi, so close after the two sisters had spent some sixty-odd years away from each other.

Camellia noticed Katherine staring at their mother's picture. "Kat, are you ok? You seem far away in your thinking".

Katherine started reminiscing about when she and Naomi were young and how they would stay outside to catch fireflies with their grandfather on his farm. "We would sometimes play for hours and hours, just the two of us. We were thick as thieves!" she said, remembering those times as if they were yesterday. But then, she seemed a little melancholy, "After Naomi and her family left Chenneaux, I really missed her and wondered if we would ever see each other again. The love of sisters is such a wonderful blessing, and my heart is filled with knowing I have at last found my Mi-Mi." Her heart felt whole again.

Camellia was touched by Katherine's reminiscing of her sisters and how happy she was to have finally found Naomi. Magnolia expressed to Katherine how glad they were to know she would be reunited with her sister. She added, "We are a fiery bunch, but I honestly do not know what we would do without each other's love and support. Having my sisters with me throughout our lives has been the most precious thing to me." They both hugged Katherine, and Camellia began to pray for the reuniting of all the sisters and the blessings yet to come.

CHAPTER 12

"SISTERS"

Camellia offered drinks to everyone. After the situation calmed down, the sisters told Katherine how happy they were for her. They understood how precious the sisterly bond was. They had always been together, except when Azellia went away to Howard for school. They had laughed, cried, disagreed, and reconciled, which is the exact thing that sisters do. They understood how important and sacred their sisterhood was, and they were grateful that God had restored their bond. He had reunited all of the sisters, giving them another chance at having and creating lifelong memories. They hugged Katherine and poured love and hope into her. She was elated and anticipated speaking with her sister.

Just at that moment, Trey's phone rang, and all he heard was crying and shouting. "Thomi, is Grand-Naomi ok? What is happening?"

Thomi was so excited, "Say man, it's all I can do to keep her from trying to get on a plane! She has been dancing around here like she's twenty years old! She asked, 'Look at the lady, does she have a mole on her nose?'"

Trey turned to Katherine, and with excitement in his voice, he said, "Yep, she sure does!"

Before Thomi could respond, Naomi took the phone. "Hello, hello, Trey put her on the phone. Now, Trey! Put her on the phone!"

Trey handed the phone to Katherine. "Kitty Kat, is that you? Is that you, Kat?"

Katherine screamed, "Mi-Mi, yes it's me. Lord!!! It's me, Mi-Mi!!!" There was joy and jubilation! The sisters had been reunited under the most unexpected circumstance. God had kept his promise to Katherine. Her prayers had been answered. *Thank you, Lord.*

After about an hour on the phone, the sisters hung up reluctantly. Thomi told Trey he would get their grandmother on a flight in the morning. He said his wife Frie would accompany her there since he had to work and could not get away until the weekend. Trey was excited and told Thomi he'd see him later. Katherine hugged Trey again. "Trey, you are my great nephew. Do I have more nieces and nephews?"

Trey began to explain the family tree that Kat never knew she had. "Well, my mom is Grand-Naomi's only child. Her name is Carletta, named after my G-Pops, Carl. Unfortunately, he's deceased. Mom married my dad, William Langston II, and had me. She already had my older brother, Thomi. Thomi has a wife named Frie and a daughter named Emerald. We call her Emmy. My dad and mom live up near Boston. Grand-Naomi did not want to live up north, so when she started to have heart issues, Thomi moved her to Atlanta with him and his family. Now that I actually SEE you, yes, you and her look a lot alike. Her hair is white as snow and she is still beautiful. She's feisty as ever, too. I sense that same spirit in you, ma'am."

Katherine laughed and said, "Yes, we were two of a kind. We were very close. I did not have as close of a relationship with BethMae because she hardly ever came around. I just remember her being tall, with large eyes like our father's and long curly hair. She was much older than me, so we really did not have anything in common. I do remember that the other children would always call her "Chocolat"[3] because she was a little darker than us. She could really sew and would sometimes make things for Mi-Mi and me. We called Naomi Mi-Mi back then. She was a feisty one," chuckled Kat.

"She had many fights about Beth Mae. She defended her when the kids were mean. Back then, darker skin was like a curse. She was the darkest of most of the Boudreaux cousins and I think she felt like she did not belong. You know back then color was important to some, but our grandfather never showed any kind of difference to her. Some would say he actually favored BethMae out of all of his grandkids. LORD!!! I am so thankful! I cannot believe that after all this time, I have finally found my family. I will get to lay my eyes upon my dear sister... TOMORROW, Lord!!! Thank you, Jesus!"

Soon after, Camellia started clearing the dishes and getting the kitchen back in order. Magnolia came into the kitchen and asked if she needed help. Camellia was getting emotional and said to Magnolia, "Sister, what a blessing for Kat and her sister. I

---

3 Pronounced *Sha-Coo-La*

could not help to think to myself, what if we had become totally estranged from Zell? What would our parents have thought? I could not bear that, Sister. And I am just so grateful that God allowed reconciliation for us."

Magnolia was also touched. "My dearest sister." Magnolia whispered to Camellia, "no matter the storm, we will always be together. We've gone through our trials and we have prevailed victorious. We are Devereaux women and we will always be the strong women our parents raised us to be. We will always rise!" Magnolia hugged Camellia and told her good night as she headed home. There was a sense of peace surrounding the Devereaux grounds. The sweet smell of lavender in the air was Camellia's confirmation that all was well.

Later that night, Trey told Katherine that he would pick Naomi up and bring her straight to her tomorrow. Katherine begged to go to the airport with Trey. Francois chimed in and said they all would go. He and Azellia would drive her and Trey to Baton Rouge. "Trey, just come here tomorrow and meet us here, we'll leave about noon. This has been an extraordinary evening. It's overwhelming to say the least," he exclaimed. He had a lot to take in as well since it looked like this side of his family was about to double in size. But until then, he looked at his new, younger cousin, put his hand on his shoulder, pulled him into an embrace, and said, "Well, Trey, welcome to the Guidry-Devereaux family!"

The next morning, Katherine was up bright and early. She couldn't sleep as she realized how much her life would change. Between her son getting married into such a wonderful family and now finding Naomi, who lived just three hours away from him, she had some decisions to make. She called her friend, Mena, in Texas to tell her the exciting news. "God is a promise keeper,

Cher! Never did I imagine I would find my sister. I constantly prayed that I would someday find my family. I came here for Francois' wedding and to meet his bride and her sisters. Never in my wildest dreams did I ever think I would be reunited with my sister. Yes Cher, God is a promise keeper!" She told her friend that she had no idea when she would return to Texas. But Mena was happy for her and told her not to worry about anything. Just be happy and enjoy her family.

Breakfast was ready and on the table. Camellia came downstairs singing, smiling, and praising God for the miracle He had bestowed upon Katherine. "Kat, what is that divine smell?"

Katherine was taking the casserole from the oven. "It's one of my dad's favorite recipes. It's a jambalaya breakfast casserole and it's to die for. I noticed andouille in the freezer yesterday, so I used some to make this wonderful masterpiece."

They both laughed and hugged and began to set the table for breakfast. "How many for breakfast, Mell?" Katherine asked.

"Oh, it's just us and Schaffer is stopping by to pick up those papers for Magnolia, so set one extra." The table was beautiful, and the food from the Devereaux House kitchen was smelling delicious. Katherine had fresh flowers from the garden in the center of the table. It reminded Camellia of when her beloved Amellia was alive and how she'd have fresh flowers all over the house.

"Today is a grand day!" said Camellia. "We are all excited about meeting your sister. She will stay here with us. I made sure the room was ready to receive her. Miss Carrie has prepared the room with fresh linens and everything she needs to feel right at home. I will be home when y'all get back. I have two meetings with my students today, so I must get to work straight away after breakfast."

Camellia waved goodbye from the driveway, and as she was nearing the gate, she said to herself, *"If it is to be, it shall be, show us so that we can see."* She thanked God for what He had done, reuniting her and her sisters and bringing Katherine and her sister together as well.

Francois and Azellia came for breakfast. Francois explained to his mother that Azellia had to go into the office but would be back about noon with Trey, and they would leave for the airport. Katherine was so happy. All she could think about was seeing Mi-Mi and hearing everything about her life and what she had been doing all these years.

Anticipation was almost getting the best of her. She cleared the table and cleaned the kitchen. She began to get herself ready to be reunited with her sister. She was saddened that BethMae had transitioned many years before and they did not get the chance to reunite, but she was grateful and thankful that she still had her Mi-Mi. It also brought her peace to know that BethMae lived a long, happy life with her husband despite the difficult life she was presented with earlier in her life. BethMae, being of darker skin, had faced many challenges growing up. Katherine remembered painful memories of what her oldest sister endured because she was darker than her and Naomi. She never really had the kind of relationship BethMae and Naomi had because they lived in separate households. Katherine lived with her mother and their dad, while BethMae and Naomi lived with their mother. She remembered all the beautiful dresses and aprons BethMae would sew for her and Mi-Mi. That memory brought a big smile to her face as she reminisced on how they would dress alike and go into town for everyone to see!

Katherine sang all the way to the airport. She was in a state of joyful euphoria. However, as they got closer, she began to get nervous with anticipation. She told Trey beautiful memories of her and Naomi's childhood. Trey was still shocked to learn of Katherine since Naomi never spoke of her. She talked only about BethMae. *Was there more to the stories of joy and happiness that Katherine shared? Was there some dark secret keeping Naomi from ever mentioning Katherine?* When Trey spoke to his Mom, Carletta, the night before, she had many complex scenarios about why Naomi never spoke of Katherine. Carletta was just as shocked to learn of her other aunt and told Trey not to press his grandmother for information. She would speak on it when she was ready.

Chapter 13

"Secrets"

As they entered the airport, the noise and traffic congestion were slightly unsettling to Katherine. "My Lord, this is a busy place! It will take days to find Mi-Mi."

Trey took Katherine by the hand and explained to her that they wouldn't have any problems and to rest assured she would be seeing her sister shortly. They waited and waited until Trey saw a familiar face. "Emmy, what are you doing here? I thought your mom was coming?"

"Uhh, hello my handsome uncle. Greetings first, sir," she replied jokingly, followed by a gigantic hug.

"I'm sorry, little beautiful one. We are all just so excited about this reunion."

"I know we've been up all night talking with Grand-Naomi. But yes, my mom is assisting Grand with her stuff. Look, here they come."

At that very moment, Katherine said, "There she is! There's Mi-Mi!" The two sisters hugged and cried and cried and hugged all the way back home. Katherine did most of the talking while Naomi studied her face non-stop.

After about thirty minutes of non-stop chatter, Katherine asked Naomi whatever happened to the judge's grandson. Naomi said in her proper Southern voice, "I married him." Katherine looked as if she was in disbelief. Then she said," After all that, you still got married?"

Naomi slowly replied, "Yes, and believe it or not, we were married almost forty-five years, until his transition."

Katherine was quiet for at least three minutes. Francois, still driving, wondered, *Who was this judge?* She finally spoke when he asked her if she was okay. But instead of replying to him, she looked at her sister and asked, "Mi-Mi, how old were you when you met Carlton? After the judge had such a fit about y'all, I assumed y'all never got back together. I was thirteen? I remember hearing our father talk about the judge as his "common" family. I never knew what Daddy meant by that."

Trey could see his grandmother becoming agitated with the conversation, so he changed the subject. "Emmy, what have you been doing with yourself? I know you're still in the modeling game because we saw your photo spread in Ebony. Girl, let me hold something," Trey laughed.

"I'll let you hold my hand, Unc!!!" That got a laugh from everyone.

As they approached the Devereaux plantation, Naomi recalled memories from when she was a little girl. "Oh my Kat, this place looks like our Papa's place in Cheneaux County. You can smell the lavender! Kat used to run up and down the backyard, smelling the lavender bushes and pulling flowers, and getting

76

scolded every time. She was determined to always have lavender in her hair."

"Yes, I have fond memories of our Papa, but I want to hear more about your life with Carlton Douglas. Girl, I would have never believed it! You and Carlton barely knew each other, I thought."

Naomi pushed her hair from her brow and looked at Kat, "We'll talk about the past when we've had a few cocktails, Sister. For now, let's leave it at that."

After that was said, everyone was intrigued and wanted to know what the "issue" was with Katherine, Naomi, Cheneaux County, and their secrets. Trey called his mom as soon as they got back to the Devereauxs. He told her there was "something" between the sisters, but Naomi seemed reluctant to discuss it. She would only do so in private with Katherine. Carletta told Trey not to push for any information. "Mother will speak on it in her time."

Dinner was divine, and everyone was feeling very full and comfortable. Camellia told Naomi, "Your suite is ready for you. I hope you enjoy the room. It was our mother's favorite suite in this old house. Katherine's room is right next to you, so y'all can be up all night chatting." Naomi thanked Camellia and said she was going up after she finished her Grand Marnier.

After pleasant chatter, the sisters retired upstairs. Everyone was curious about what the conversation would be about, but only the sisters would be privy to that! Naomi thought to herself as she was getting ready for bed, *Life is so funny. Who would have thought I would be reunited with my baby sister after all these years?* She heard Kat knock on the adjoining door. "Yes, Kitty-Kat, come on in."

Kat immediately laid on the bed and said, "Tell me everything Mi-Mi. I want to hear it ALL!"

CHAPTER 14

"DECISIONS"

Naomi stared in the mirror. She finally spoke. "Kat, so many things were happening with my mother and BethMae. With the state of BethMae's mind after losing Jules and not ever being able to have children, it was quite a bit to deal with. She lived in a constant state of depression. She loved Jules with the deepest part of her heart. My mother did the best she could, and when she realized that BethMae needed something different, she had to do what was best for her. That's why my mother decided to let BethMae move away. Papa Boudreaux told our dad and my mom to let her leave and go stay at the farm in Cheneaux so that she would have a chance at a new life and happiness. I hated to see her leave, and shortly after, my mother decided we would move to Ford County, never knowing that that was where Carlton had gone."

Katherine sat up and said, "Why did they send Carlton away? What happened to Jules had nothing to do with him. Jules was hot-headed and very jealous. No one better not ever look at BethMae for too long or they'd have a fight on their hands. Jules was determined to make his own way and not do what his father and grandfather wanted him to do. He was strong-willed and bull-headed. The drinking and bad behavior was a direct reflection of how he felt about the 'uppity Douglasses.' He hated them! It's bizarre that he felt hatred towards his family, while Carlton was the opposite."

"Carlton adored his family," she continued. "He had his mother's sweet spirit. They made sure Carlton had whatever he needed, but Carlton never gave them any problems. He was the perfect son, while it seemed Jules did everything he could to be bad. He could have had anything he wanted. He chose to be bad, even passing for white when it suited him and then always causing some sort of altercation when he said he was black. Jules chose his own path, it's just sad that his actions had such an impact on BethMae and all of us, for that matter. It's so sad that his temper got the best of him in the end. Mi-Mi, you were hot-tempered back then too, remember?"

Naomi raised her brow and replied, "Back then? Oh my beloved, then and sometimes even now, but time has mellowed this lioness' heart," she laughed, shaking her head. "Well after Jules died in the wreck, they shipped Carlton to Ford and everything changed. That was a horrific wreck. It was a miracle BethMae survived. Everyone said God had BethMae in His arms protecting her. After hitting the bridge, the car burst into flames. That's why it is still a mystery till this day that she survived. After her recovery, BethMae was about to have a nervous breakdown, so leaving and going down to Papa's farm was the best medicine for her. But she was never the same. She wasn't able to have children due to injuries she sustained from the car accident. It took her quite a time to recover physically, but mainly mentally. Jules killed, and then her not being able to have children, was just too much. But she found happiness in Cheneaux. She met a wonderful man and they had a long happy life," she said bittersweetly. "Okay," she continued, "enough about that. I don't really like talking about the past. It disheartens me."

Katherine, with her large eyes as bright as headlights, said to Naomi, "One more question, Sister, and I will lay it to rest. Whatever happened to Benson, Carlton's younger brother? He was such a handsome boy."

"Benson moved to Ford about a year after we did. He lived with Carlton up until we got married. He is still in Ford, as best I know. Retired and "living the life of Riley," Naomi chuckled. "Carlton and I became very close when BethMae left," she reminisced. "I guess him missing Jules and me missing BethMae drew us close. Once we got to Ford County, and I realized that Carl was there, it made the sadness of having to leave everything I knew seem less and helped me cope with not having BethMae with us. Carl, as he went by in Ford, worked hard and gained status quickly. We dated for about two years and got married."

From the look on Katherine's face, Naomi knew the next question was coming. "Yes, Kat, I was pregnant, but no one knew except my mother and Papa Douglas. We were married quietly and started living our lives together in Ford, away from all the sad memories that we all held. Actually, it was our new beginning. Carl and I had a wonderful life in Ford County. No regrets, little sister, other than not being able to be with you.

We had one child, a beautiful little girl. Our daughter grew up in a loving home, we gave her everything you and I never had growing up. She's married and has two fine young men, Thomi and Trey. You'll get to meet Thomi soon, as well as her loving husband, William. They reside in the Boston area, but I suspect she will be making a trip to the South very soon," they both chuckled.

"Life was great until Carl got sick," she revealed somberly. Katherine had tears in her eyes, witnessing her sister's pain. She slowly reached for Naomi's hand and then embraced her. "It was the most difficult time in our lives. We shared almost fifty glorious years and not one regret. God was merciful to us, and for that, I am grateful. I'm excited for you to meet Carletta. She looks so much like Carl's mother. It's almost eerie, and everyone used to say I had her for his mother."

"Anyway, we owned a small grocery store and Carl worked for the city," she continued. "After his father passed, Papa Douglas willed the Douglas House to Carl and me and we made our life there. We had great times and some sad, but we had a good life. We were prominent and had the respect of everyone in the county. When he passed, everyone from across six counties showed up to pay their respects to my beloved husband. We had a wonderfully blessed life, with no complaints and certainly no regrets."

Katherine's large eyes were filled with tears. "Oh now, Kit-Kat, no need to fret, sweet Sister. I am content with the life I had and with the life I have now. Carlton and I had a lifetime love, as it says, until death do us part. And I am good! I got my family and now, you. I am blessed." They hugged. "And after a lifetime, we have been reunited through the most unlikely circumstances. You have a son, a very handsome son - he has Papa's ears," they both laughed and continued to reminisce about the past well into the evening. Life had not always been kind to the sisters. Like the Devereaux sisters, the Boudreaux sisters had seen sad, devastating times of loss. But at this point along their journey, God had blessed them immensely with reuniting their families and letting them both know that life was good.

CHAPTER 15

"LIFE GOES ON"

The following morning, they awoke to the smell of pure divineness! Camellia had the house smelling like her mother's famous breakfast buns. You could smell the rum as you entered the kitchen! "Good morning family. I trust everyone slept well. We've had quite the reunion and it's just an absolute blessing," she exclaimed, elated with joy as she spoke and almost sang her words. "Francois and Zell are coming by for breakfast. They need to talk about something. Probably about business, I suppose."

Just as Katherine was coming downstairs, they arrived. "Well, good morning to the Guidry's," she stated. "Ya'll sure are in a festive mood."

Azellia cleared her throat and asked where Magnolia and Miss Naomi were. "They will be down in a second. I heard Maggie on the phone so she should be wrapping up," responded Camellia. "Zell, you look so pretty this morning, almost glowing. Is that a new foundation? I must get into town. I need my hair done badly. It's a mess! I'm really thinking about getting it cut. There are so many new styles now and I want something cute and sassy!" laughed Camellia.

Magnolia and Naomi came down the stairs together. Naomi told Katherine, "Kat, look at your daughter-in-law. Look in her eyes, Kitty-Kat. What is it that Ma-Ma Olivia used to say? '*There is a glow to behold, and it is life.*'"

At that moment, Katherine screamed at the top of her lungs, "OOOOHHHHH, my God! Y'all are pregnant, aren't you? Aren't you?"

Azellia was shocked! *What in the world?* "HOW did you know, Miss Naomi?"

Katherine grabbed Azellia, hugged her, and just started praying, saying her life was complete, she was happy, God was good, and life was grand! It was the most joyful minute any of them had experienced! Magnolia and Camellia were crying and just ecstatic with joy. The Devereaux legacy was living on, and everyone present felt the love and joy in the house on THAT day! Everyone was so excited they nearly forgot about the delicious breakfast still awaiting them. There were questions and questions and more questions. Magnolia stated, "Well, she will have to go to Mary Magdalene Sacred Heart. That's a given," she laughed.

"And then Dillard, right Zell?"

"We do not know yet, sister, what we will have. But girl or boy, we will allow our children to make their own decisions. But of course, with our input," declared Azellia with a wink. She and Francois smiled so fondly at each other. This baby girl or boy would always have the best of everything! Devereaux, Guidry and Bordeaux. What a bloodline indeed!

Azellia and Francois wanted to discuss what being pregnant meant in terms of her continuing duties at the Devereaux Corporation. Azellia despairingly confided to the sisters that this was actually their second pregnancy and that she had miscarried about seven months prior. No one knew that Zell and Francois went through that loss alone. Magnolia looked at Azellia in disbelief. Camellia immediately embraced her and told her how sorry they were. Magnolia sat by her youngest sister and asked, "My sweet Zell, why didn't you tell us? Those were times when you needed us most. I can only imagine. I'm so sorry you felt you had to bear that alone. We will always be here for each other. No matter the quarrel or disagreement, we will always be by each other's side. Always. Whatever the storm, we will weather it together."

Azellia had already told Schaffer to meet them for breakfast at the Devereaux House. Schaffer Comier had taken on a more visible role as Chief Legal Officer and was capable of handling all of Azellia's clients' legal needs. However, she could not take on the day-to-day operations of the job. Schaffer had suggested that the daily operational duties be given to Trey. He was dynamic and knowledgeable, and everyone respected him because he had proven wise beyond his years on several occasions. Francois was also becoming more and more fond of Trey as well and had the utmost confidence in his abilities to do the job.

Magnolia and Camellia agreed that Trey was the right choice to temporarily replace Azellia during her pregnancy. They also agreed that his performance had shown that the company would be in capable hands. Magnolia asked when they would present this to Trey. Francois said they would like to have dinner on Friday to give them time to work on their proposal for him. Schaffer would also be present to ensure all bases were covered.

Katherine and Naomi were up early Friday morning preparing for the dinner. Naomi told Katherine she was proud of Trey and knew his parents would be just as proud. She said she wanted to call Carletta and let her in on the new job offer, but then she promised she would be patient so Trey could make his own announcement. Katherine said, "Mi-Mi, isn't God amazing? Look at how He has blessed these two families, the Devereaux and Boudreaux sisters. His amazing grace has brought us together at a time in our lives when we can still enjoy each other and our children and their children."

"Yes, Kit-Kat," Naomi said, "We are blessed. No matter what we've gone through in our lives, the heartache, the loss, and the triumph, God has always gotten us through to joyous ground. And Kit-Kat, you are about to experience the greatest love of all, being a grandmother. My dear, sweet Sister, your life is about to change in the most amazing way!"

CHAPTER 16

"WHEN THE RAIN HAS PASSED...AND THE MUD HAS CLEARED"

E veryone was awaiting the Guidry's new arrival. They were all excited. Camellia decorated the nurseries at the Devereaux House and Azellia's and Francois's home. They were ready to receive Little Miss Amellia Katherine Devereaux Guidry!

Naomi and Katherine were excited about cooking dinner on Friday night. Devereaux House had an aura surrounding it. The lavender seemed more aromatic than usual. The sun appeared brighter, and joy and elation abounded. Camellia requested a driver to take her and the Boudreaux sisters into town to the market so they could gather what they needed for dinner. With this being a two-fold celebration, Camellia suggested surf and turf, jambalaya, string beans, and key lime pie to top it off.

After discussing the proposal with Schaffer, both Azellia and Francois felt comfortable with their presentation for Trey. Francois had told Trey to be at the Devereaux House at 7:00 pm for dinner because they had a business proposal to discuss with him. He did not give him a clue about the tremendous opportunity he would be presented with. He sensed the anticipation in Trey's voice and assured him it was all good!

After a long day at the market, things were coming together in the kitchen, and you could smell the deliciousness miles away. The sherry and mushroom steaks were about to peak with the perfect center as Camellia removed them from the oven. She said, "These must rest so that the flavor will settle. The shrimp and crabs should be ready in a few minutes. Kat's divine salad is beautiful, and Miss Naomi has made the most heavenly vinaigrette. Let's journey to the parlor and await our guests. Schaffer is coming, too. This will be a most spectacular evening. It will be the dawn of new beginnings, with endless opportunities and bountiful blessings!"

Trey was not only prompt but twenty minutes early. He was a little nervous and anxious, too. He brought beautiful flowers for the sisters. "Miss Camellia, I know you love flowers, so I brought these in hope that they may grace your lovely table."

"Oh my, that was so sweet, Trey." His grandmother Naomi was in the corner, encouraging him and giving him unconditional love.

"Well, Grand-Naomi, I could not come empty-handed. Mom and you both taught me that," he said, knowing she would expect the best from him.

"Come Trey, everyone is in the parlor. Join us for a small cocktail before dinner. I am sure that a libation will calm your nerves, young man. You do drink, don't you?" quizzed Camellia.

"Maybe a glass of wine every now and then, but that's about it. I must admit that I have grown fond of sweet tea since I've been down South." Trey laughs.

"Well, whatever suits your fancy, I'm sure we can accommodate your taste," stated Camellia.

Francois greeted Trey with a firm handshake. Trey reciprocated, of course. Francois was so impressed with his little cousin and wanted to bring him into their fold straight away. He motioned for him to go outside on the porch, away from all of the chatter in the parlor. He wanted to talk to Trey and explain what was happening so he could process it and be ready to give his answer after dinner. After Francois finished, Trey looked at him and said, "Are you for real, sir? Are you kidding me? This is already like my dream job, but to be offered such an opportunity, I am beyond grateful. YES, sir, I will gladly and with honor take the position. Mrs. Guidry has been great to me, and if this is my chance to show her and the Devereaux family how much I appreciate them, I'm ready to roll with it!" They shook hands, and the deal was done.

"Ok everyone," Mell called out to the group. "Dinner is served, so come on in." Once they were all settled at the table, she asked, "Trey, would you like to say the blessing over supper tonight? I think it's very appropriate for you to do so, if you agree."

"Yes, ma'am, Miss Camellia, it would be my honor," stated Trey. Trey blessed the food, the evening, and the family that brought his Grand and her sister together. He was intentional in his prayer, which moved Magnolia and touched her heart.

"Well, you certainly are a fine young man and you'll make a welcomed addition to this family, Trey. We welcome you and your family to ours. Cheers to new beginnings and endless opportunities," toasted Magnolia.

Dinner was divine. After it was over, Schaffer suggested that they begin their presentation for Trey. Azellia and Francois explained the scenario to Trey and laid out everything regarding responsibility and compensation. He was overwhelmingly surprised and grateful and accepted the terms of the proposal. He exclaimed, "Wow, I am honored and humbled that y'all have faith in my ability to handle things for Miss Azellia. I accept the challenge and I will do my best to keep the Devereaux Corporation running smoothly and efficiently at all times! Thank y'all so much. I promise to make all of you proud."

By this time, Naomi and her sister were both in tears of joy. They were both so proud of Trey. Azellial raised her glass and toasted, "Trey, may your days be filled with joy and anticipation for each opportunity that comes your way. May God keep His hand on you and continue to bless you in exceptional ways. Congratulations, Mr. William Thurgood Langston III! Welcome aboard, counselor!"

God had a plan all along, but bringing it to fruition was everyone's job on the journey. From the amazing encounter with Azellia and Francois, through the most difficult situations between the sisters, and to reuniting two separate and distant families into one, God was always in complete control!

The Boudreaux and Devereaux sisters had all come full circle, so to speak, in one way or the other. Going through so many challenges and heartbreak, they survived it all. They were entering a new phase of their lives together as one big family. New generations, new legacies, endless opportunities, and abundant blessings were ahead for these two families, now united as one!

As the mud clears, washed away by the sweet rain, all is forgiven, and the union of the Boudreauxs and Devereauxs heralds a new legacy as they become one family. Blood is indeed stronger than the "mud"!

The End

...or is it just the beginning?

"If it is to be, it shall be, show us so that we can see."

Epilogue

Just as Camellia pulled the drapes, she thought, *What a beautiful full moon. This will be a magical night.* As she turned out the light downstairs, the phone rang. It was Magnolia.

"Sister, meet me at the hospital, Francois and Zell are there. She has been experiencing unusual pains, so Francois decided to take her to the hospital."

Immediately concerned and hearing the unease in Magnolia's voice, Camellia said, "But it is not time, is it, Sister? We anticipated at least three more weeks. We are still preparing the nursery."

Magnolia stated, "Sister, you know as well as I, the full moon brings about new life. So yes, it is time. Gather Kat and Miss Naomi and come quickly."

Katherine and Naomi could hardly walk fast enough. Poor Camellia was exhausted trying to keep up with them. "We are here for the Guidry family, where are they?" Katherine asked excitedly. The nurse pointed them to the waiting room.

Magnolia was there, looking both worried and excited. "What's happening?" inquired Naomi.

"Well, she is in a birthing room, so we should have a new baby hopefully before the morning," Magnolia replied. Katherine was elated and started crying, while Camellia immediately started praying.

The sisters were all together, awaiting the arrival of baby Guidry. Katherine and Naomi sat together on the waiting room sofa, holding hands and talking about how wonderful life was and how God himself made everything possible: their reuniting, their new life, and now, another generation to love and celebrate.

Magnolia could see Francois coming down the hall and immediately got up and ran halfway to meet him. He looked almost pale, which startled her.

"Francois," Magnolia said firmly, "what is wrong? How are Zell and the baby? Is everything alright?"

Francois looked at Magnolia with tears, saying, "Babies, not baby, babies - there are two of them."

Katherine jumped up in disbelief, "What did you say - two? Oh, my God! Mi-Mi, did you hear? There's two of them. Oh, my God!"

Francois said the doctor had explained that if they did not maneuver themselves for a normal birth, a cesarean might be warranted. He then hurried back to the birthing room to be with Azellia.

Camellia asked where the chapel was, and the nurse took her there. Once in the chapel, she lit a candle and began praying. "Oh, Father Mother God, we know You are in control. Give us what we need to help Francois and Zell through this. Touch those sweet babies and guide them to us. We trust You, and we know *if it is to be, it shall be, show us so that we can see.*"

Two hours passed, and it was about 11:30 pm. Katherine was the first to see Francois running down the hallway. "They are here! Our beautiful, sweet little girls are here!" She and Naomi were crying. Magnolia and Camellia were hugging, and Francois was overcome with joy!

Katherine and Naomi had witnessed the greatest love of all. Seeing their legacies continue and prosper and watching their children become one family was the greatest gift either could imagine. They felt blessed and could feel their sister BethMae looking down on them as their lives moved forward with so many blessings. But it wasn't just them who felt this way.

Camellia and Azellia were awed to see Magnolia soften and open herself up to all of the happiness around her, which was clearly beneficial to the entire family. And for Magnolia, seeing her nieces for the first time melted her heart. She embraced the situation with love and gratitude. But only time would tell if she'd opened her heart enough to accept what lies ahead for her.

Camellia was overtaken with emotions. She told Magnolia that she wished their mother was still in the present to witness this, but she knew she was there in spirit, with a full and happy heart. She smiled at the babies, her two little nieces, and said, "Now, on this beautiful full moon night, God has sent two little angels to change our lives. They are our future. Only You, God, knows what the future holds and we look forward to Your work with anticipation."

Recipes from the Sisters

This book is filled with discussions of wonderful, delectable food from the South. As a special treat, we have included four recipes that we hope you will enjoy. Food is definitely the love language of the South. These are some of our favorite family recipes passed down through the ages, with love, tradition, history, and always a great story behind each one. Close your eyes and open your pallets to these savory Southern dishes we know you will enjoy. We guarantee that they will become favorites of your family as well.

"Laissez le bon temps rouler"

AMELLIA'S OLD FASHIONED BREAD PUDDING

Bread Pudding

- 1 loaf of stale French bread, cut into 1-in cubes (about 6-7 cups)
- 2 12-oz cans evaporated milk
- ½ Cup Water 4 brown eggs
- 2 c sugar
- 3 T vanilla extract
- ¼ c Grand Marnier
- 1 c raisins (soaked in 1/4 c Grand Marnier for about an hour)
- ½ t cinnamon
- ½ t Nutmeg
- 3 T unsalted butter- melted

1. Preheat the oven to 350 F, place milk, water, and ¼ c Grand Marnier in a large mixing bowl, and add the bread that has been cut into squares. Press the bread into the mixture with your hands until all the liquid is absorbed.
2. In a separate bowl, whisk the eggs, sugar, vanilla, nutmeg, and cinnamon. Pour over the bread. Add the Grand Marnier-soaked raisins and gently stir to combine.
3. Pour the melted butter into the bottom of a 9 x 13-inch pan, and coat the pan's bottom and sides well with the butter. Pour the mixture into the pan. Bake at 350 degrees for 35-45 minutes or until the liquid has set. The pudding is done when the edges start getting brown and pull away from the edge of the pan.
4. While the bread pudding is cooking, make the Grand Marnier sauce.

Grand Marnier Sauce

* 1 stick butter, melted
* ¾ c. sugar 1 T flour
* 1 c. Half & Half
* 1 T vanilla
* 1 tsp nutmeg
* ¼ - ½ c Grand Marnier *(depends on your mood)*

Melt butter and flour in a medium saucepan on low heat for about 5 minutes. Stir in sugar, add half & half, and cook for about 3-5 minutes. Add vanilla and nutmeg. Slowly cook over low heat, stirring constantly until the mixture thickens. Then remove from heat. Don't allow the mixture to simmer over heat. Whisk in the liqueur to taste. Whisk the sauce again before serving. The sauce should be soft, creamy, and smooth. The bread pudding should be served with sauce on the top or, if preferred, on the side.

Big Momma's Mac N' Cheese

- 1 pkg small elbow macaroni
- 1-2 cups half & half
- 8 oz shredded sharp cheddar
- 8 oz shredded colby jack
- 4 oz shredded smoked gouda
- 4 oz shredded mozzarella
- 4 oz sour cream
- 4 oz cream cheese
- ¼ cup bread crumbs
- 1 brown egg, beat a little
- ½ stick butter

Preheat the oven at 375 degrees. Prepare pasta as instructed on the package. Rinse and drain. In a large bowl, mix macaroni, 4 oz shredded sharp, 4 oz shredded colby jack, all the rest of the remaining cheeses, with all ingredients except bread crumbs.

Mix well until all cheeses are blended and creamy. Add half of the bread crumbs. Mix well. You might need more liquid; if so, pour small amounts and stir until desired creaminess. *Only you know if you want creamy or dry mac and cheese so add liquid accordingly.

Spray a casserole dish with non-stick cooking spray. Pour the mac mixture in the dish. Sprinkle with remaining bread crumbs and remaining sharp cheddar and colby jack shredded cheese. Bake at 375 degrees for about 30 minutes or until the cheese has melted, golden brown and bubbly.

SOUTHERN GIRL COLLARD GREENS WITH SMOKED TURKEY

- 6-8 bunches of Collard greens *(depending on the size) 3-4 smoked Turkey Butts
- 2 bay leaves *(Remove before serving)
- 1-2 cups chopped Trinity **(onion, bell pepper,celery)
- 4-6 cups Chicken Broth ***(make your own or use granulated Chicken Broth mix)
- ½ tsp Soul Food Seasoning ****(whatever kind of seasonings you like)
- ½ tsp granulated garlic
- 2 -3 fresh jalapeno peppers, chopped fine
- ⅓ cup sugar

Cook turkey butts overnight in a crockpot. Pick and wash greens thoroughly. Roll greens up and cut into strips. Put turkey and juices into a large stock pot, add greens and all ingredients. Bring to a high boil. Reduce heat to a medium boil and cook for about 2 hours or until greens are soft and tender. You may need more liquid throughout the cooking process. Add chicken broth and seasonings to suit your taste. Let simmer for another hour.

Down South Dirty Rice

(or Rice dressing - depending on where ya from)

- Small package chicken gizzards (about 8-10) Small container chicken livers (about 8-10)
- 2 T margarine
- ½ lb ground beef
- 1 lb pork sausage (like breakfast sausage) 1 c. chopped onions
- ½ cup chopped celery
- ¼ cup chopped bell peppers *(onions, celery and bell peppers are referred to as "The Trinity)*
- 1 tsp minced garlic
- 2 T chopped fresh parsley
- ¼ tsp ground thyme 1 tsp salt
- ½ tsp black pepper
- ½ tsp crushed red pepper
- 4 cups cooked parboiled rice **(Use 4 cups water and 4 cups chicken broth to cook the rice - gives it a richer flavor. Cook in a rice cooker for perfect rice.)*

Preheat the oven to 350 degrees.

Place gizzards in a pot and add enough water to cover. Bring to a boil and let boil for 10 additional minutes. Add livers to the post and continue to boil for another 5 minutes, until water is about boiled out. Set aside.

In a heavy pot, melt margarine. Add ground beef and sausage and mix together well. Add the trinity and garlic. Let cook over medium heat.

Remove livers and gizzards from water, chop them up very finely. ***(Use a chopper if you have one - less stress on those old bones.)* Add to meat mixture and continue to cook for 15 - 20 minutes, until meat and seasonings are married together. Add parsley, thyme, salt, crushed red pepper, and black pepper. Stir mixture well.

Stir rice into the mixture. Mix it very well. Pour into a 2 quart baking dish.

Bake in the oven until brown - about 25 minutes.

.

www.ingramcontent.com/pod-product-compliance
Lightning Source LLC
Chambersburg PA
CBHW070042030726
47506CB00003B/829

* 9 7 9 8 2 1 8 3 0 9 0 9 1 *